Praise for *Th*

Opposite worlds and conflicting desires clash in this action-packed, page-turning suspense.

Richard Paul Evans
#1 *New York Times* Bestselling Author
The Christmas Box and *The Walk*

The Patent freakin' rocks! Extremely well written, it is a can't-put-it-down story. Awesome. There is a sequel, right?

Michael Enos
Chief Financial Officer

The Patent is sheer genius! It's not only riveting and thought provoking, but has more twists and turns than a habit trail. An unapologetically modern man's thriller.

Katie Leigh
Author of *Adventures in Oddity*
and *Voice of Your Childhood*

In *The Patent,* co-authors Max Garwood and P.S. Wells take the reader on wild ride full of intrigue, betrayal, and family turmoil to the brink of World War III. An edge-of-your-seat page-turner that will keep you enthralled to the very last page.

Henry McLaughlin
Award-winning Author
Journey to Riverbend

Technological espionage, the race for state-of-the-art weapons, gun smuggling, blackmail, kidnapping, and murder–*The Patent* has everything to keep you saying, "Just one more chapter… just one more."

Debbie Wilson
Christy Award-winning author
Tiger in the Shadows

Civilization as we know it is at stake. If you are a reader who wants strong characters on a complex journey that has you asking "Why?" and "How?" over and over, here's the story for you. Garwood and Wells know their craft. Well done!
David Pierce
Author of *Don't Let Me Go*
and *To Kill a Zombie*

Just finished your new book, *The Patent*. Couldn't put it down! Amazing!
Christine Sacco Williams
Educator and Activist

As an actor, I live for great stories and this is one! Nothing better than an intriguing spy story and *The Patent* has all the components of a great one. Great story, great characters, all put together by a great writing team!
Gary Moore
Actor

The Patent

One Weapon Will Make Your Enemy Invincible

P.S. Wells
Max Garwood

Pegwood Publishing

Title: The Patent, Revised edition
By P.S. Wells and Max Garwood
ISBN: 978-1-7331060-1-6 (paperback)
       978-1-7331060-2-3 (ebook)

Subjects: 1. Fiction/Action & Adventure
2. Fiction/Thrillers/Suspense
3. Fiction/Thrillers/Espionage

Cover photo: nOahKEaton, 99designs.com

Published by Pegwood Publishing
Roanoke IN 46783

Printed in the United States of America

Dedication

To our readers.

And to Max, Barbara,
Marquis, Sarah, and Evan

who have become family.

P.S. Wells

Chapter One

Shanghai. He hated the place.

Busy and overpopulated, the city offered plentiful opportunities to remain anonymous, a necessary convenience for Colonel Jai Yao's business. China's most populous city and one of the first to adopt the one-child population control policy, Shanghai presented the sadistic illusion of prosperity to countless peasants that immigrated from country villages. The place also bore cruel memories that haunted his sleep and confounded his waking hours.

The dirty military vehicle dropped him in front of a tired looking building. One of many religious structures confiscated by the government, the former temple now belonged to the people. The People's Republic.

Most of these historic structures served as Custody and Repatriation Centers. In an effort to "clean up her cities," China rounded up beggars, street children, garbage gatherers, prostitutes, the homeless, and any unregistered workers. Anyone authorities opted to bully.

Inside, Yao processed through a security checkpoint. Under vaulted ceilings, the place smelled of age and centuries of incense burned during religious ceremonies.

Passing an oversized room, sweat broke out on his top lip. Barely lit by narrow windows set far above a man's head, he remembered a similar place, years ago. Reeking of sweat, that room had been jammed with prisoners, all charged with the unpardonable crime that they did not belong. Yao didn't belong.

Insufficient ventilation in the overcrowded space left the inhabitants lethargic, their eyes dulled by hopelessness. Some lay curled on the filthy floor, seeking relief from intestinal complaints. All were plagued by pest infestations and desperate for access to toilets and water for washing.

He shook his head to push away the memory, reminding himself that this building had an entirely different purpose.

In a concrete-walled corridor at the building's center, two guards flanked oversized double doors.

Again, Yao flashed his identification, and the doors opened. What had served as the temple's inner sanctuary currently resembled a laboratory not unlike the one where he had studied on the other side of the world. Like the lab at the Massachusetts Institute of Technology in the United States, the overhead lights were bright, and the controlled air circulated cool and dry. Wearing white lab coats, two-dozen Chinese scientists and technical personnel were busy at workstations.

"Colonel Yao." From the center of the room, one man broke away from his task and came quickly to Yao's side. "We are honored by your presence."

The Colonel barely acknowledged the simpering department supervisor. "Walk with me."

The two passed one workstation after another. Colonel Yao viewed each with a critical eye. "Tell me about your progress."

Chapter Two

Marc Wayne grabbed a fire extinguisher and doused the greedy flames. His eyes stung, and fire erupted a second time. Emptying the contents of the canister, he ignored the chirp of his cell phone.

At last, Marc and the extinguisher prevailed, and the flames died. Just to be certain, he stood at the ready, poised to combat another fiery outburst. When nothing happened, he relaxed and set his weapon on the granite kitchen countertop next to the television. Movement on the screen caught his attention, and he turned to the news channel report.

"In a grab for military superiority, the Chinese leap-frogged the jet engine technology of the free world. This new Chinese engine powers a superior model fighter plane that, according to the National Security Adviser, 'poses a serious threat to the safety of our borders.'"

While the news reporter narrated, the flat screen showed a video clip focused on an expanse of sky. As Marc watched, a jet appeared and sliced through the clouds as seamlessly as a dolphin cutting through surf. "Nice."

The CNN report changed topics, and Marc threw open windows to vent the smoke and fumes. He swept the disappointing remains of his invention, dumped the ashes into the kitchen sink, and flushed the mess down the disposal.

Letting the faucet run, Marc mentally recalculated the inter-connecting ingredients and the sequence of steps that should have produced an adhesive. As he purged his flopped experiment down the drain, he kept one ear tuned to the TV. The morning news predicted overcast skies.

"Weather guessers." He gathered his hair into a ponytail and switched off the television.

On the routine bicycle ride downtown, Marc cycled through the neighborhood where he'd grown up, past welcoming homes with front porches for sitting out. He peddled leisurely, hearing his bike wheels crackle over the early September leaves swirling along the sidewalks and pooling against the curb. He wheeled around a corner and biked down Main Street. Past the bank, funeral home, and the Veterans of Foreign Wars Post, he braked in front of a narrow brick building that once served as the post office but had been divided vertically into two narrower offices. The sign read *Marcus Wayne, Patents*.

Leaning the bike against the sign, he heard the phone inside. He fished his pocket for the key and unlocked the door. But the ringing had stopped. Recalling the year he was twelve and had worked his first paper route, he picked up the morning newspaper. Today's front-page wire story asserted that rapid advancements in military superiority by governments hostile to the United States could be a precursor to World War III.

"Mornin', Marc." A gravelly voice called. "Did you see the news?"

Marc turned to see Dr. Thurmond Yoder peering over his glasses. As long as Marc could remember, Thurmond had been the local veterinarian. The building's landlord, Dr. Thurmond, housed his practice in the west section and rented out the east side.

"How's business, Dr. Thurmond?"

"Barking along." The wizened old man appeared tall, thin, and angular, like the brick office they shared.

"Glad to hear that."

"I'm glad to hear anything at my age."

When Thurmond had an especially mouthy Chihuahua hospitalized for several days, Marc understood why this rental space had been available so often. "And just how old are you, Dr. Thurmond?" Marc welcomed their customary morning repartee.

"Old enough to remember when you used to come in to get your hair cut."

Marc tossed the key inside where it landed on the receptionist's desk. "I was five."

"Business was slow, so I took up dog grooming. I was clipping your dog, and you asked if those clippers worked only on dog hair."

"And you said, 'Let's see.'"

Thurmond wagged a finger at him. "Looks like you could use another trim."

"Obviously, the experience traumatized me." Marc shook his head. "Haven't been able to face a set of clippers since."

"I might have medication for that."

"I'll keep that in mind." Marc threw a casual salute. He started into his office, but his neighbor called him back.

"About the news?"

Marc nodded. "I saw the new Chinese military jet engine."

"Read today's top news story." Dr. Thurmond pointed to the newspaper in Marc's hand. "During World War II, I served as crew chief aboard the aircraft carrier *USS Monterey*."

Marc knew the story. Well. While a teenager, Dr. Thurmond lied about his age and enlisted, making him one of the younger veterans of that war. "Along with future president Gerald Ford who helped you fight a fire below decks."

"Fire erupted from colliding aircraft when swells caused by Hurricane Halsey tipped the ship 70 degrees. During that December of 1944, we lost 147 planes and 490 men." Dr. Thurmond removed his glasses and cleaned them with his vet smock. "Do you see the connection?"

Like when he got caught daydreaming in school and the teacher called on him, Marc felt unprepared for the question. "Connection?"

Dr. Thurmond held up his glasses and examined the lenses for smudges. "World War II stood as a clear case of good versus evil. Enslaving force against republic liberty."

Unsure what to say, Marc shifted his weight.

"My generation fought fiercely with the technology we had." Dr. Thurmond slipped the clean glasses back on and studied Marc. "What will you do about this new threat?"

"Me?" Marc felt like he wanted to loosen his tie, but he wasn't wearing one. Didn't even own one. "Or my generation?"

"Every generation needs leaders. Especially when the wolf growls at the door." With a nod, Dr. Thurmond disappeared into his vet clinic.

Marc opened the morning paper and balanced the pages across his bicycle's handlebars. Scanning the disturbing cover story, he pushed his bike inside and kicked the door closed behind him.

In this small Midwest town of Dixon, Indiana, Marc felt insulated from the world's conflicts. These new political developments had nothing to do with him. Surely, someone else would handle the global situation. Someone else always did.

Chapter Three

Special Agent Mallory Wayne checked the time and mentally rehearsed her argument.

"Relax." Her partner, Thomas Brenau, joined her at the conference table.

"I'm fine."

"Then stop twirling your hair." He tugged at his own short-cropped crown. "It makes you look like a novice." He snapped his fingers. "Oh yeah, you are the newest member of the task force."

Mallory shifted her twirling into a quick scratch behind her ear. "Welcome back from maternity leave. Have photos of that new baby?"

"Introducing the reason I was out of the office, so you got to be the lead on this project." Thomas unfurled the photo section of his wallet like an accordion. "Meet the third Brenau production."

"People keep *albums* on their computer."

"I can show you those, too." He opened his cell phone where a photo of his wife and children served as the screen wallpaper.

Already talking, Special Agent in Charge, Logan Deverell entered the FBI conference room. Early forties, he sported a deep tan and a perpetual cup of coffee. "Talk to me, people."

Mallory opened her mouth to open the meeting, but nothing came out. Her carefully prepared introduction vanished from her mind.

Thomas cleared his throat and indicated the overhead screen. A wide-faced black man reared in Georgia's historic Savannah,

Thomas had just celebrated his thirty-fifth birthday. The counter-
terrorism specialist took the remote from Mallory's hand and
pointed the device at the overhead screen. "Here's the segment of
the CNN special that started this parade." The news clip described
a specialized jet engine manufactured by an Asian company and
marketed to governments hostile to the United States.

More than a decade younger than her supervisor, Hoosier
native and Purdue graduate, Mallory specialized in research and
analysis. She saw her moment to re-engage. To take charge.
"According to Department of Defense analysts," Mallory gestured
toward the now silent screen, "that engine is an obvious copy of a
General Electric engine under development for a new Boeing
fighter/bomber."

"That explains why the Defense Department has their
underwear in a wad." Deverell unwrapped a stick of cinnamon-
flavored gum. "Our directive is to stop the flow of industrial and
defense sensitive information to foreign entities."

Mallory passed a file to Deverell. She opened her own copy
and began to read. "Going back over the last two decades, Hsu
Kai-lo and Chester H. Ho, naturalized citizens, were arrested by
the FBI in June 1997 and charged with attempting to steal the
process for culturing Taxol."

Deverell raised an eyebrow. "Taxol?"

"Used to treat ovarian cancer." Mallory leaned forward. "A
trace element found in an endangered species of yew tree used in
the formulation of the drug. Bristol-Myers Squibb invested
millions to develop the process for culturing commercial quantities
of the material from plant cells."

Thomas added, "A federal grand jury returned indictments,
eleven counts against Hsu, Ho, and a female accomplice, Jessica
Chou."

"Hsu, Ho, Chou?" Deverell waved at the stack of files in
front of Mallory. "Sounds like verses from *Old MacDonald Had a*

Farm. With a ho-ho here and a chou-chou there… What else you got?"

"In August 1997, Harold C. Worden pled guilty to felony interstate transportation of stolen property. A 30-year employee of the Eastern Kodak Corporation, Worden worked as project manager for a processing machine using a secret formula that determines the quality of the photographs." She slid that file to the bottom of the pile and opened the next one. "Kuxuhe Huang sent US trade secrets worth $300 million to China and Germany. Charged under the 1996 Economic Espionage Act, which passed after the US realized China and other countries were spying on private businesses."

Deverell held up his hands. "Okay. Got it. That stack holds how many such case examples?"

Thomas fanned his own stack with his thumb. "I make it to be the size of a DC phone book."

"Heavy on the research and evidence, Mallory." Deverell swept his hand in an exaggerated motion, indicating the number of files. "What's your point?"

"The point is that we have agents doing a good job tracking down industrial espionage." Mallory tapped the files with a manicured index finger. "The successful development of that jet engine by the Asian company is the result of vital information secured before the Air Force tested the engine. Before the theft ever became another case of industrial espionage."

"Before?"

"General Electric worked on the design, using strict security precautions. The functionality of the GE engine showed up in foreign hands before GE made the design public." Thomas emphasized the word 'before.' "The guts of this engine were disclosed in several patent applications that GE filed to protect the design for later commercial development."

"Meaning?"

"Meaning." The moment had arrived to press her leadership and display her analysis and deductive reasoning on this case. Mallory spoke each word with overstated slowness. "Somebody had access to the functional design before GE had the engine tested."

Deverell frowned, thinking this over.

"Nor was the engine reverse engineered," Thomas added, "since there are none on the market."

"Like Americans did to the sturdy and utilitarian German motorcycle during World War II, giving us the Harley Davidson." Deverell smiled. "My personal favorite piece of stolen technology."

Thomas smirked. "Yeah, we saw the new model in your parking space."

"Boys and their toys," Mallory noted flatly, eager to get back to her findings.

"So, we know what it's not." Deverell finished his coffee. "What do you have for moving forward?"

Quickly, Mallory handed a second file to her boss. "Patent applications are screened upon receipt at the USPTO—"

"Us-pee-toe? Are we back with Old MacDonald's farm? Speak English."

"United States Patent and Trademark Office. Patent applications that might impact national security are referred to appropriate agencies for consideration of restrictions."

Deverell chewed his gum. "And then?"

"If the agency concludes that disclosure of the invention would be detrimental to national security, the Commissioner for Patents issues a Secrecy Order, withholding the publication of the application of the grant of a patent as long as national interest requires."

"Congratulations, your genius idea is now a military secret." Deverell tossed his empty coffee cup into the trash. "Every pencil pusher has his moments of glory. Okay, so much for the boilerplate. What's your theory?"

Thomas nodded to Mallory. She read encouragement in his eyes.

She squared her shoulders. "Secrecy orders were issued for the GE patent applications relating to the fuel delivery and control systems for the engine." To slow the nervous rush of words, Mallory took a deep breath. "The only disclosure of the design outside of the security perimeter was by way of patent applications that revealed the conceptualization."

Deverell looked at his watch. "And the bottom line?"

She set up her theory like setting up a three-point basketball shot. "Our theory is that the information in those applications was compromised in the patenting process."

"Before," Thomas emphasized.

"Before General Electric delivered the first engine to the military?" Deverell reached for a pen on the tabletop. "What about leaks at the GE plant?"

Mallory shook her head. "The fuel delivery and control systems were developed by separate teams."

"The plot thickens." He clicked the pen several times. "Meaning?"

"Only the Patent Office had all the applications together in one place." With every click, Mallory's nerves tightened. She glared at his pen.

Deverell followed her gaze and clicked the pen faster. Louder.

"The common denominator," Thomas looked from Mallory to Deverell, "is the Patent Office."

"Thomas and I suggest that we investigate the possibility that the information flow begins at the Patent Office. That's our starting point."

"Is there an echo in here?" Deverell loudly chomped his gum.

Mallory felt herself flush at the jab and plunged on. "Particularly patent applications stamped with a Secrecy Order."

"Ah—security's weakest link," the supervisor clicked the pen, "is the individual."

Mallory and Thomas nodded.

"Your suggested plan of action?"

Mouth suddenly dry, Mallory wished for a stick of Deverell's gum. "Let's submit our own patent application for an invention desirable for military applications. The goal is to trace the information channels."

Deverell stood and gathered his files. "Find the leaks. Shut them down, and while you're at it—quite frankly–get some good PR." Halfway out the door, he called back. "Eeeny, meany, miny-mo, catch a Hsu, a Chou and Ho. Work out the details, people. Back here in the morning."

Chapter Four

Tim Saad massaged his temples. Maybe some coffee. Someone said caffeine cured headaches. Or was that another American saying? What did they call them? Urban legends?

Stopping at the restroom, he checked his sugar level and gave himself an insulin shot. In the break room, he reached for a cup and stepped aside as one of the support staff joined him at the coffeepot. His employer, the United States Patent and Trademark Office, employed more than 8,000 people at the huge five-building campus headquartered in Alexandria, Virginia. More than half were patent examiners. Fewer than 500 were trademark attorneys. The others were support staff.

"Hi, Tim." The pert woman had skin the color of his coffee with just the right amount of cream.

He held his cup under the coffee urn and flipped the lever. "Hello."

"How are you?"

The pot was empty. "Apparently too late for coffee." Though he couldn't remember her name, he did remember it was Hispanic. Being an agency of the United States Department of Commerce, the Patent Office resembled the San Francisco airport, with half its inhabitants being foreign nationals. He pressed a thumb against his temple. "And this headache is distracting."

"I know what you mean." She stepped closer. "Taking a walk helps. I like to go to the atrium. For the view and some vitamin D."

"Vitamin D?"

"Sunshine." She waved her hand toward the ceiling. "Natural lighting instead of the indoor kind combined with blue computer screens."

"A walk." To keep his sugar level balanced, his doctor recommended regular walks.

"I walk every day. Why don't you come with me?" She rested a hand on her slim waist, her fingernails shiny and red tipped to match her lipstick.

In his fifties, Tim guessed the pretty woman to be twenty years younger. He looked at his watch. It was break time. He nodded his thanks, and they set off in the direction of the atrium.

Once downstairs, she pointed him toward the current display. "You go ahead and take in the new hoopla. I've seen it already. I'll meet you on the other end with coffee."

Protecting Intellectual Property was the new exhibit featured in the Patent and Trademark Office Museum housed in the impressive Madison Building atrium. The timeline illustrated the history of patents and trademarks in the United States.

A plaque described, "Currently based in Alexandria after a 2006 move from the Crystal City area of Arlington, Virginia, the office has been fully funded by fees charged for processing patents and trademarks applications since 1991. The move to the new complex came under the leadership of Under Secretary of Commerce for Intellectual Property, Jon W. Dudas, appointed by President George W. Bush in 2004."

Tim considered the modern USPTO campus and marveled at the equally immense revenue generated by intellectual property applications. Awarded in 1421 to Filippo Brunelleschi for an improved method of transporting goods up and down Florence's Arno River in Italy, the first patent encouraged the spread of knowledge while protecting the inventor's legal interests.

The unlimited ability of the human mind to create provided a constant source of amazement. This building stood as a credit to minds that had designed a process to amass income from the abstract ideas of others. Developed and maintained by the National Inventors Hall of Fame, the museum and gift shop were favorites of tourists. For Tim, an occasional visit reminded him of the bigger picture, a view of the end product of his efforts.

Born where poverty and starvation shadowed everyday life, Tim grew up with the understanding that doctors and engineers were respected. Government positions carried prestige. Now employed with the United States government, he was respected and admired, at least in his native land. Patent examiners, like him, were generally scientists and engineers. Tim's bachelor's degree in mechanical engineering qualified him for his examiner's position, but his proclivity with electro-mechanical devices placed him in the art unit that examined electrical/mechanical devices.

Further along, the exhibit addressed the Invention Secrecy Act of 1951, "designed to prevent disclosure of new inventions and technologies that, in the opinion of selected federal agencies, present a possible threat to the national security of the United States."

Tim leaned closer. Like a writer finding a review of his latest book, Tim read on to see how the exhibit described his particular responsibilities. "The Department of Defense, military agencies, the National Security Agency, Department of Energy, NASA, and the Justice Department provide a classified list of sensitive technologies that earn an invention a secrecy order."

Reading the same information, a tourist pressed close. Tim moved farther down. "A secrecy order requires that the invention be kept secret, restricts the filing of foreign patents, and specifies procedures to prevent disclosure of ideas contained in the application."

Smelling of spicy kimchi, the tourist bumped against him. Annoyed, Tim moved to the next section. "The types of inventions classified under this Act are a secret. By the end of 2007, there were 5,002 secrecy orders in effect."

He looked sideways to see if the tourist without regard for personal space might be bearing down on him, but the man had disappeared. So had Tim's pesky headache. Checking his watch, he noted that break time would end soon. Tim hurried his pace to the end of the exhibit. As promised, his co-worker met him with two steaming cups in hand.

She smiled as he approached. "Here you go."

"Thank you." Tim sipped the strong brew.

"I took the liberty of adding sugar." She stirred her own cup and tossed the spoon into the trash. "Low blood sugar can cause annoying headaches."

She remembered a lot about him. Perhaps they had spoken at the Christmas party. Her name still eluded him.

"Feeling better?" They began walking back to their floor.

He nodded.

"A walk," she confided, "can be life-changing."

Chapter Five

As usual, he arrived before his secretary. Marc tossed the newspaper next to the nameplate that let visitors know the pretty lady that occupied the receptionist desk was Violet Seiwert. He parked his bike next to the oversized pottery crock that served as an umbrella stand. In colors of clear and turquoise, unmatched porcelain and glass insulators from abandoned power and telegraph poles were mounted on the wall and served as pegs for his coat and scarf.

Down the hall, Marc passed his own office in favor of his workroom at the rear of the building. He dropped his backpack on the worktable, slid open the zipper, and set several objects and a legal pad filled with scrawled notes on the already crowded surface. He snapped on the tabletop light and bent over his project.

That's where Violet found him later in the morning. He knew she had arrived when the overhead office lights came on. Moments later, he recognized the honest fragrance of his favorite Earl Grey tea.

"Did you check your email?" From the kitchenette, he heard the ting of a spoon as it stirred. That would be the honey she laced in the morning's tea.

He didn't bother to look up. "Go ahead. Let me know if there's anything important."

She came into the room and peered over his shoulder. She smelled of spring lavender. "How's it coming?"

"In the tinkering stage, but looks promising."

Violet set his John Deere mug near his elbow. "Here, hot and steamy. Cream and honey, the way you like it."

"By the way. Could you pick up another fire extinguisher?"

"I sent a new one home with you last night."

"Yes. You did. Good thing, too." Marc added a note to his yellow pad. "And I need another one."

"Hmmm. Perhaps I can arrange a quantity discount." She turned to leave but stopped at the door. "This isn't another ice cream scoop, is it?"

He sighed. "You wound me, Violet. I patented that while still a teen and sold it to Ronco."

"Or a hairbrush that removes static electricity?"

He glanced at her from under his arm. "And used the static to cause the brush to glow. Very cool." He returned his attention to his project. "I patented that design, too. Which led me from electrostatics to electro-magnetics."

"Magnets."

"Magnetic field sensors and superconductors and the Meissner Effect."

"I see," she said, and they both knew she didn't. "All these inventions, yet, you can't work the teapot."

"That's why I need you, Violet."

She snorted. "You need me for a lot of things—" The phone interrupted her.

"Including answering the phone." Marc's elbow bumped the mug and sent it crashing to the floor where it shattered, sending ceramic shards scattering, and Earl Grey splashing across the room.

The phone rang again as they both eyed the damage.

"That's the phone." Violet hooked a thumb over her shoulder. "I'd better get it."

Chapter Six

A letter awaited Yao when he returned to his home. Simple by Western standards, his house was larger and nicer than most. The housekeeper had left the mail in a lacquered tray on the entryway table. The correspondence from his parents arrived like clockwork. Pouring a cup of pale-colored tea, he scanned the contents.

"The medicine you sent eases the swelling in our joints and the pain the winter cold brings." He recognized his father's careful handwriting and pictured those old hands that once skillfully nurtured fledgling plants. The previously long and slender fingers were now bent, gnarled, and crippled.

Jai Yao recalled his years growing up as a peasant farmer's son in a poor farming village situated in China's countryside. Each year, a traveling preacher arrived. Thin and gentle, the preacher was nameless except that the villagers called him Brother.

"Brother is here," the villagers had whispered as they passed each other in the fields or carried water.

After dark, many neighbors quietly crowded into his parents' home. Yao fell asleep in his mother's lap as Brother spoke late into the night. In the morning, Yao would wake on his own pallet where his father had carried him sometime in the middle of the night. He rose and accompanied his father to the fields, feeling sleepy and always hungry. There was rarely enough food to quiet the growing boy's empty stomach.

As he grew older, Yao sensed an unspoken understanding

between the common farmers. The villagers were careful to keep the Brother's brief presence secret from the stern village cadre.

Thinking of his father's hands, Yao pictured the day he and his father were bent over, working side by side in the green rice fields. Smelling dank and promising, the earth had to be coaxed, even seduced, to produce enough crops to see them through until the next year's harvest. Suddenly, they heard screaming. Racing from the fields, Yao saw strangers throwing the few household belongings from Yao's simple home. One man held a worn portion of a Bible over his head with one hand and, in his other hand, he cruelly gripped Yao's mother. He clutched her hair by the roots, holding her head at an unnatural angle.

"This is what happens to criminals." Superiority in his voice, he yelled to the neighbors, who cringed a fair distance away.

Bolting forward, Yao quickly outdistanced his father. Head down, he barreled into the man who held his mother.

"No, Jai," cried his mother as she was thrown to the ground. The man and the teen rolled and sprawled apart. Yao sprang to his feet, ready to fight. From behind, the cadre and the other stranger grabbed him and pinned his arms. A hand gripped Yao's hair in a tight fist, forcing the boy to look as Yao's mother and father were brutally beaten.

"Stop!" Again and again, he screamed the same word. Struggling fiercely against the iron grasp that held him, his body became drenched with sweat and his own tears. He wailed until he had no more voice. At last, the attackers exhausted their rage.

Curled in a fetal position on the bloody ground, Yao's mother did not move. The men who held his father released their hold on the battered and bruised man, who crumbled to the ground like a pile of broken sticks. As the men yelled something to the horrified villagers gathered around this nightmare spectacle, Yao watched his father crawl to his wife, place a hand against her face, and sag into unconsciousness.

Those who held Yao threw him aside. A booted foot crushed his fingers, and he felt the bones snap like dry twigs.

The boy's childhood home was set ablaze along with the family's belongings, heaped into a pile like so much rubbish. And then the strangers were gone.

Chapter Seven

"The phone is for you." Violet called back to the workroom.

Marc swept the broken pieces of his cup into the dustpan and tossed the wet mess into the trash.

"It's Mallory."

Marc jogged to his office and picked up the receiver. "Hey, big sis."

"I've been trying to reach you. I telephoned early this morning and called your office."

"Yeah? What's happening in the big city?"

"The usual. Stuffed shirts wearing the same hairstyle and trying to run or ruin the country."

Dropping into his swivel chair, he glanced at the familiar words framed on the wall.

Congress shall have power… to promote the progress of science and the useful arts by securing for limited times for their authors and inventors the exclusive right to their respective writings and discoveries.
—Article 1, Section 8, United States Constitution

Next to it hung a second framed quote.

The question whether there is a patentable invention is as fugitive, impalpable, wayward, and as vague a phantom as exists in the whole paraphernalia of legal concepts.

> *If there be an issue more troublesome, or more apt for*
> *litigation than this, we are not aware of it.*
> US Judge Learned Hand
> Supreme Court

"Thinking about a trip home to Indiana?" He peered out the window. "The hot summer season is over. An early frost sent Dr. Thurmond scurrying to his garden to harvest his still green tomatoes."

The siblings knew the drill. Tucked inside brown grocery sacks and stored on basement shelves, the tomatoes would emerge for the Thanksgiving table. In Hoosier tradition, the rosy red tomatoes added vibrant contrast between the greens and yellows of green bean casserole beside deep-dish macaroni and cheese.

She sighed. "I'd love to see home in the autumn, but I've got an assignment."

"Which you can't tell me about," he mimicked in his best James Bond impersonation, "or you'd have to kill me." From the top of his broad wooden desk, he picked up a horseshoe magnet and twirled it around his finger.

Balancing a nine-iron and a collection of coarse fish nets, Violet came into the room. With creative efficiency, she threaded ecru netting onto the golf club and rested the nine-iron in the curtain rod hooks above the window. She fluffed the antique draping into place and stood back to evaluate the look. In the short time she had been working at the office, she had been steadily redecorating.

Marc wondered if a receptionist's job description included adding texture to an office. He knew he hadn't talked about that topic during the interview process. Perhaps core classes for university business majors included accounting, marketing, computer skills, and creating tasteful environments for business owners with style deficits and no interior designer on the payroll.

Did her style even have a name? The look certainly wasn't anything he'd seen before. Antique doilies framed the window by Violet's desk, artfully strung on a Queen Anne piano leg. Turned horizontally, the shapely cherrywood functioned in its second life as a window treatment. A table next to the receptionist's desk held a collector 8-track player and a stack of recordings, including Journey, Charlie Daniels, and the soundtrack for *Fiddler on the Roof.* Across from Violet's desk and smelling of furniture wax, squatted a wooden church pew for clients while they waited. A hymnal rack held several magazines.

Mallory's tone changed, and Marc knew she was getting to the real reason for her call during business hours. The two spoke often, but this wasn't just the big sister checking up on her little brother and the usual parrying of sibling witticisms. "Actually, this call is equal parts personal and business. We could use your help."

Violet adjusted her handiwork and nodded in satisfaction. From his desk, she picked up the outgoing mail and left the room.

"Does my country need my expertise as a small-town patent attorney or one of my world-changing inventions?" He passed the u-shaped magnet over a stack of ferrite magnets. Absently, he observed the attraction of the two elements. Rotating a rectangle magnet, he intuitively measured the distance until he felt them repel.

"A little of both."

He swiveled his chair for a better look outside. "The autumn colors are your favorite shade. Grape, orange, and lemonade, as you used to name them." Marc did not add that the view looked better with his receptionist's fresh framing. "You can have whatever you need in exchange for a visit home."

"Are you bribing a government official?"

He flipped a ferrite magnet into the air and caught it with the horseshoe magnet. "Negotiating, baby. Negotiating."

Chapter Eight

In the weeks following their beatings, neighbors gave generously of their limited medical supplies and carefully nursed Yao's parents. Despite kind ministrations of herbs and oils, their injuries were severe, and the boy knew they would never be the same. He kept busy doing what he could while his broken hands healed.

And he did a lot of thinking. The Brother came from somewhere else and departed to another destination. The sadistically wicked men who brought destruction were not from any of the nearby villages. They were well dressed and well-fed. Yao had heard of other villagers who traveled away from the quiet countryside fields into the large city of Shanghai, where jobs and food were rumored to be plentiful. Unable to eke out a living for the three of them here, the boy knew his only option was to venture to the city.

Without a goodbye, because he knew his parents would not want him to go, the teen set out on foot. Days later, he spied Shanghai on the horizon. The throng of humanity crowded together among the immense buildings stunned Yao. But even with countless people in one bustling place, he struggled to find work in this unfriendly setting.

Going from shop to shop in a retail district pungent with odors of food and waste, Yao offered to do any odd jobs. He worked diligently at any task, hoping to prove his worth and find consistent work. He wanted to fill his own rumbling stomach and save money to take back to his parents.

Suddenly, chaos broke out. Around him, people yelled and ran. A group of men dressed like the ones who descended on his village appeared in front of him. Instinctively, Yao spun around and ran as fast as he could, his feet pounding up and down like pistons. He dodged shoppers and shop owners, and leapt over merchandise.

Glancing back, he felt relieved to see he had navigated plenty of distance between himself and his pursuers. He knew he'd get away.

Until he crashed headlong into two policemen.

Chapter Nine

For several hours at his desk, Tim concentrated on a particularly intriguing application. All patent examiners were under a strict quota system since the office had received public criticism for customarily taking longer than a year to process patent applications.

An accelerated examination procedure had been implemented, promising patent applicants a speedy evaluation of their submission. Most applications were filed electronically, and filing fees were paid by credit card, putting patent hopefuls in the queue at a rapid pace.

Checking the time against his progress, he felt his headache return. Thinking back to his walk through the exhibition at lunch, he decided to purchase a pain reliever at the museum gift shop. He stood and stretched. Reaching for his wallet in his back pocket, he felt surprised to find an envelope. Turning the envelope over, he tried to understand how this came to be in his pocket. Sliding his thumb under the edge, he tore open the flap.

From inside, he removed a sheet of paper folded around a photo. The clear image showed three men. They were sitting atop a cliff overlooking Israel's Salty Sea—the Dead Sea, as the Americans called it. One swarthy Bedouin poured Turkish coffee into the small cup of a second Bedouin. The second man's face was visible, and Tim recognized him from news reports as an arms dealer.

Taller than the other two, the third man in the picture trained a pair of high-powered binoculars toward the distant mountains of Jordan. Tensions between Israel and Jordan were high, and unsavory men used this to their advantage. For a bribe, Jordanian border guards didn't object when someone crossed their border illegally into Israel's Negev wilderness.

Looking at the tall man, Tim studied the picture closely, gasping for some relief from the panic that surged within like a storm on the Mediterranean coast. Suddenly, his shirt felt too tight, and he wiped his moist palm on his pant leg.

Without a doubt, Tim recognized the tall man. Tim's adult son, his only son.

A second photo lay behind the first. Sweat from his hands made the two stick together. Again, he wiped his palm on a pant leg and fumbled at the thick corner to pry the first picture from the second. What he saw caused his knees to buckle, and he dropped into the office chair. The same three men were gathered around a stack of rectangle boxes. The lid had been crow-barred off the top of a wooden crate to reveal Kalashnikov AK-47 rifles.

The son of a Muslim man and his Jewish wife caught trafficking illegal arms amid the boiling cauldron of friction in the Holy Land. Action would be swift and public as an example to others—and depending on who got to him first—torturous.

With trembling hands, Tim turned over the photo, but there was nothing on the back. Searching the envelope, it was empty. Smoothing the folds of the white paper that had enfolded the picture, he found a lightly penciled message. "I'll be in touch."

Chapter Ten

Tucking the first of his father's carefully and painfully scribed pages behind the second, Yao paused to pour hot tea from the pot into his half-full cup. The contents had cooled, and he detested tepid tea. While always welcome, these letters from his devoted parents occasionally triggered undesirable memories. He lifted the cup to his full lips and drank, his eyes no longer seeing the letter but a time many years past. Back to the day the police had caught him in the marketplace.

Along with a dozen others who didn't run fast enough, Yao had been transported to an old building that looked out of place among the modern structures that flanked both sides.

"A temple!" one prisoner exclaimed, relief in his eyes.

"It's a temple, all right." A policeman grunted and shoved Yao and the others toward the majestic doorway. "Welcome to the new religion."

Inside, someone crammed the teenager into an already full cell and locked the door behind him. In time, the teen learned he had been detained as one of the three no-haves: no papers, no job, and no abode. Detainment was arbitrary. Once each day, food arrived, though the meals were low quality and never enough. Without medical attention, skin infections, lice, and sickness were quickly widespread.

Each day, Yao went to a work center where he and the others were forced to labor to pay for their room and board.

"Eight yuan for daily food." The guard ticked off the list on his fingers. "Ten yuan for daily management for three no-haves personnel." He poked Yao in the chest. "If you don't like it here, you can be transported to another Center for 200 yuan."

"I don't have money."

The man gave him a toothless sneer. "Your family can pay what you owe."

Yao stared at the man, trying to make sense of the senseless situation. Then the guard pushed him into the vermin infested cell.

Despondency settled over the prisoners in the Confinement and Repatriation Center like a sodden wool blanket, pressing from them hope and life. Several prisoners were taken away. Rumors were murmured that these poor souls went to work prisons. They'd be worked to death and die in obscurity. Another whisper reported prisoners that disappeared were executed, and their organs harvested. Their fate would be a mystery to their families who would never hear from them again.

Yao convinced the work camp's supervisor that he would do the work of two men if the tally would be applied to his account. But after several days, Yao realized his wages were not being doubled. Exhausted and angry, he returned to dragging through a regular day's tasks.

When the work supervisor was berated for the drop in production, a wink told Yao he would receive extra if he worked like two men. But the food rations remained the same.

As Yao's concentrated efforts began to reduce his bill, he encouraged the other detainees to use more effective and efficient methods. Production improved, as did the attitude of his cellmates, though they were still starving. Expending more energy than they took in, the workers grew thin, but Yao didn't see another solution to their impossible situation.

One day, the guard took Yao to a room. A man in a military uniform looked him over and asked questions. Another man in a white lab coat passed endless tests under Yao's nose until his eyes wanted to cross. When he had enough, Yao threw the pencil at the coated man and went for the door. At that moment, the military man uncovered a tray and told the teen he could have the food piled onto the dishes in exchange for more tests.

For the first time that Yao could remember, his belly felt full. He ate every morsel and sped through the next wave of simpler tests. Pointing to the boy's protruding ribs, the man in the military uniform offered an opportunity to be schooled and trained. And fed. When the man assured Yao that his parents would be provided for as long as he remained loyal, the teen accepted.

Later, in school, he realized the second battery of tests was probably no easier than the first batch. After eating, Yao's blood sugar reached a level that allowed him to think and reason with ease. He determined he would never be hungry again. And he would find a way to improve his nation, so that no one in his country must be hungry as he had been for most of his life.

Chapter Eleven

The rest of Tim's afternoon passed in a blur. His emotions
darted like a wild bird caught indoors. Who had taken the photos?
What did they want? What about his wife? Though years, cultures,
and an ocean separated them, he still loved her. Was she in danger?

As he made his way home after work that evening, his
thoughts chased each other like mice on a wheel. Approaching his
front door, he tentatively reached for his keys, afraid of
discovering another unwanted surprise in his pocket.

"Hello." The cheerful voice made him jump. The small girl
who lived next door appeared at his side. She was nine years old,
Tim recalled. Her family had invited him to share birthday cake
some months ago. In preparation for the birthday celebration, they
had conspiratorially deposited a small kitten into Tim's care that
Saturday morning.

"I just picked her up from the pet store." The girl's mother
pressed the soft bundle of sleeping fur into his hands. "It's the one
she's had her eye on. Could you keep the kitten here while we put
the party together? Then bring it over with you. I want to surprise
her."

Before he could protest, the young mother had flitted off.
"Don't tell," she called back.

Tim had looked dumbly at the kitten dwarfed in his palms. To
his relief, the two of them spent a companionable morning
together. He sat on the couch and watched television while the tiny
visitor slept in his lap. When the kitten woke, she had followed

him, playfully batting at anything that moved while he went about his usual weekend chores of laundry and tossing forgotten leftovers from the refrigerator.

In the afternoon, he had picked up his small charge that immediately fell asleep again in his grasp. Making his way next door, he became an instant hero when he produced the now purring birthday gift and placed the kitten in the hands of the beaming birthday girl. Since that day, the kitten often met him as he returned home in the evenings, rubbing against his leg as he collected his mail, mostly junk with a sprinkling of monthly bills, and unlocked his door. Then she disappeared back to her own address. On the weekends, the neighbor girl frequently wheeled the kitten past in a baby stroller, the sleepy-eyed cat content under a lace baby bonnet.

"Hello." Tim put out a hand to pat the nearly grown cat purring in its young owner's embrace.

"She has a new collar." His neighbor shifted the cat in her arms so Tim could admire the addition.

Tim scratched the cat behind a small ear. "Looks like she likes it."

"Yep." The little girl bounced on her toes. "See ya' Mr. Tim." And she skipped away.

Expecting someone to appear at any moment, Tim remained jumpy all night. By midnight, he decided the mysterious visitor would choose his own time to make contact. But sleep eluded him as he tossed restlessly on his bed, chasing answers and his blankets.

Certainly, the ill-mannered tourist had slipped the envelope into his pocket. The man who pressed too close and smelled of chorizo. How long had someone been lurking, watching, waiting to pass the photo to Tim?

Whether his son had been merely exploring the Negev and stopped for coffee with Bedouins or had become involved in smuggling, whether the photo was staged or not, wouldn't matter. The image would be enough to inflame zealots to murder.

Chapter Twelve

Like a drought-ridden field soaks up rain, the young Yao had eagerly absorbed his studies provided by the state. After graduating university, his benefactors sent him to the United States to attend MIT.

In modern Boston, surrounded by a host of the most brilliant minds on the planet, he learned that the population of his homeland neared two billion. The population of the relatively newer United States tallied a mere three hundred million. Yearly in China, 20 million children were born, and six million people died for a net increase of 12 million. China's population tripled since the founding of the People's Republic in 1949. Shanghai served as home to nearly 13 million of his country's people that congregated there.

On the darker side, each year, China arbitrarily detained two million people. A shocking 20 percent of those were children. Over 900 million people in his native land lived in rural locations and made less than one dollar a day. Like he had. Like his parents before him. With his belly full for the first time in his life, he determined to do something about the sparse situation his family lived in and the abysmal conditions he experienced in the C&R.

With an advanced degree in Computer Science and Artificial Intelligence, the graduate traveled home for a visit with his parents. Though unable to work to provide for themselves, they were once more living in a simple home and, for the first time in their lives, had sufficient food.

"You are a fine son," Yao's father had said. "You have honored us by taking good care of us in our old age."

In the village, Yao implemented systems for clean water and improved irrigation for the fields. Until Major Gao's car had arrived to take him back to the city.

"We have invested a great deal in you," the older man began, and Yao knew this meant he owed his benefactors. What he owed the People's Republic. His service would ensure his parents lived in safety.

Now, finishing his tea, Yao folded the letter. He placed the message in a drawer along with the other letters that had come before. Each correspondence reassured him that his parents were cared for. Each letter reminded him of what his government expected from him. And each letter renewed his desire to make his country, and his people, powerful.

Chapter Thirteen

The next morning, Tim drove his usual route south on Jefferson Davis Highway. At Duke Street, he turned right, followed by a left onto Holland Lane, and a right onto Emerson Avenue. He motored into the shadowed parking garage and turned off the engine. As he reached for the door handle, the passenger door suddenly opened, and a man slid onto the passenger seat.

"What do you want?" Tim tried to keep his voice steady.

"You've been expecting me." Small, humorless eyes bore into his. "Good."

"Who are you?"

The man waved away the question. "I will trade the life of your son—your only son—for something of equal value to me."

"But—"

"Quickly. I am not a patient man."

"You can't—" Tim gripped the steering wheel to still his trembling hands. "I have nothing you'd—"

Like a striking snake, the man's hand flew to Tim's throat. The sinister grip tightened, crushing his windpipe. Releasing the steering wheel, Tim clawed at the man's sinewy forearm.

With his free hand, the attacker drew a spring-assisted tactical knife and pressed the honed blade against Tim's throat.

Like a terrified bird, Tim's heart hammered in his chest. With difficulty, he rasped out, "What do you want?"

"Every day you are privy to patent applications that the rest of the world cannot view."

"I can't just—"

Pressing the blade harder against Tim's throat, the intruder's sour breath filled his nostrils. "I want you to give me information protected from common view."

Tim's eyes widened.

The man nodded. "I see you understand which ones I am talking about."

His pulse thundered in his ears. "But—"

"If you want your son to live, you will bring something my clients will want."

Involuntarily, Tim gave a slight shake of his head and suddenly jerked back from the sting as the knife blade deftly sliced through the skin between his nostrils. Tim's eyes watered violently.

Clutching Tim's throat tightly so that he could no longer breathe, the wiry man positioned his sharp knife above his deadly grip and slowly cut a shallow line across Tim's neck. With a final squeeze against his windpipe, the man slammed Tim's head against the steering wheel and left as quickly as he had come.

Looking to his right, Tim saw the passenger door stood open. Into his lap, drops of blood dripped from his nose and neck. Stars clouded his vision as Tim opened his own door, leaned over the pavement, and vomited.

Chapter Fourteen

Mallory had a plan she would sell this morning to her boss. During the short trip on public transit from her townhouse to work, Mallory employed the time to rehearse her presentation.

An imposing figure on Pennsylvania Avenue, the J. Edgar Hoover Building, came into view. Two days after Hoover's death, on May 4, 1972, President Richard Nixon signed a law naming the structure for the Federal Bureau of Investigation's colorful first director. From the organization's inception in 1908 until 1975, the Bureau had been housed with other offices of the Department of Justice. American entry into World War II postponed the formation of a separate edifice. In 1964, a plan was approved for 2,800,876 square feet to house 7,090 employees. Construction began in 1967. Contrasting with the neighboring marble, granite, or limestone government buildings, the poured concrete exterior contained a unique aggregate of crushed dolomite limestone.

Thirty-eight years after the first proposal for a separate FBI building, and fifteen years after Congress approved construction on the site, employees moved from nine separate locations into the FBI building. A kiosk was added in 1981. In 1991, sidewalk and trees were replaced, and a polished granite wall was adjoined to the courtyard as background for the plaque presented to the FBI by the Judicial Conference of the United States Committee on the Bicentennial of the US Constitution in honor of the Bill of Rights. The details were cumbersome, yet Mallory found the history interesting.

Arriving at work, Mallory noted the expansive building appeared starkly bland compared to its neighbors with the single exception of the 1989 panels depicting US presidents and important events during their administrations. She liked being part of world events. Though she played her part behind the scenes, being involved made her feel important. Significant.

Today, she had a strategy for stopping the information leak at the Patent Office. She collected her thoughts once more and prepared to meet with her team.

Later that morning, Deverell whistled *Old MacDonald Had a Farm* while his assistant set cups of coffee on the conference table for Mallory, Thomas, and their supervisor. She tossed two small plastic creamers to Mallory and left, closing the door smartly behind her.

Mallory opened the meeting. "Our directive is to trace the source of sensitive information leaks at the US Patent Office."

"Where are we in the process?" Deverell tapped his pen against his coffee cup.

Thomas outlined their progress. "We've contacted inventors to prepare and submit patent applications for inventions that would be desirable for foreign commercial applications. Particularly of interest to foreign military."

"These will be tracked." Mallory emptied a creamer into her coffee. "To trace the information channels, watch for the leaks, and shut them down."

"And," Deverell clicked his pen, "getting some good PR—"

"Wouldn't hurt," Thomas finished.

"What technologies are involved?"

Mallory knew the answer to this. She had established specific criteria that would yield pertinent information for their investigation. "We stayed away from current Department of Defense projects. But we want to sweeten the honey pot to attract our target."

"Submit an application that would be irresistible to a technology thief." Thomas looked back to Mallory.

This was where she unveiled her strategy. "We opted to search for an idea with military potential from an inventor completely separate from any government connection. A real person, so no one in the information pipeline would get suspicious. Someone with a plausible idea and a legitimate application."

"Does this prince charming come with a glass slipper?" Deverell tucked the pen behind his ear.

"We found a hobbyist who submits patent applications on a fairly regular basis," Thomas began.

Mallory turned to face Thomas. "It's not a hobby to him."

Thomas put up his hands in surrender. "My apologies, Mallory."

Deverell cleared his throat. "Who does he work for?"

"For himself." Mallory dumped the contents of the second creamer into her cup. "And he's a patent attorney, so he would generate his own applications."

"We're not sure if his freelance patent work for other inventors supports his inventions or if his inventions support his office," Thomas noted.

Deverell finished his coffee and tossed the cup at the trashcan. The cup hit the rim and bounced to the floor. "What does this patent attorney and semi-hobbyist inventor have that a foreign entity would be interested in?"

"The invention we selected is for a vehicle propelled by the generation of a Meissner Field." Mallory held her hand, palm side down, and circled it above the tabletop.

"A what? English people, we speak English here."

Mallory handed a computer printout to her boss. "If this could be developed, the Meissner Device would have substantial commercial and military ramifications."

Deverell tapped the paper. "So how did you technophobes

come up with that?"

"The design was suggested as being the Holy Grail of magnetic inventions by the hobbyist"—Thomas glanced apologetically at Mallory—"inventor."

Deverell scanned the information on the printout. "Wrong fairytale. No glass slippers, but knights, a round table, Excalibur, and a love triangle. Go on."

"This particular inventor," Mallory added, "is well-known for his inventions centered on electromagnetism."

Deverell looked to Thomas. "We'll assure him that the FBI simply needs the application to look realistic. The plan is to get his permission to submit and track this patent application. We'll dangle the Holy Grail and see which foreign knight comes courting."

Mallory cleared her throat. "We have his permission."

Thomas turned to her. "You've already told him what we have in mind?"

She nodded.

Thomas directed his attention back to Deverell. "We already have his permission."

"People," Deverell's voice was low, "who is this guy?"

Thomas hooked a thumb in Mallory's direction. "Mallory's brother."

The supervisor's eyebrows shot up. "Brother?"

"Her baby brother."

Deverell looked from Thomas to Mallory. "Your brother is an inventor?"

"And patent attorney," Thomas listed.

"Well," she spread her hands, "he's my adopted brother, actually."

"That explains everything." Deverell retrieved the pen from behind his ear and began clicking.

She closed the file and folded her hands. "My parents adopted him—"

"I understand that part." He clicked his pen with each word for emphasis. "You're suggesting involving family members. That move proved disastrous in Camelot."

She straightened. Ever since Marc had come home as a winsome infant, she had been fiercely protective and mother hen in love with her brother. "I recognize that. But Marc really is an inventor. He is a patent attorney known for submitting his own patent applications. This application will appear natural. Expected."

"Rather than raise suspicions, a submission to the United States Patent and Trademark Office from a respected patent attorney should not scare away our info thief."

Deverell sat back and studied the ceiling, the pen still and forgotten on the tabletop.

"He fits the profile," Thomas put in.

The boss sighed and rubbed the back of his neck.

Mallory pressed, "And he's really working on a—"

"Meissner Field Generator." Deverell thumbed through the papers in front of him.

As lead on her first project, she had given her best recommendation for moving forward with this case. Her only recommendation. Deverell would approve or reject her suggestion. Mallory forced herself to remain quiet.

Finally, he closed the folder and stood. "All right. Let's run with it." He left the room whistling *Camelot*.

Chapter Fifteen

Bent over his computer, Marc became aware of the scent of lavender. Glancing up, he saw Violet in the doorway.

"Can I get you something before I leave? Tea?"

Marc stretched. "What time is it?"

"Time to close the office." She came to stand beside his desk. "Working on another patent application?"

He nodded. "Lucky guess, considering it's what I do."

"You do a lot of things. But you most enjoy the applications."

"Really?" He rocked back in his desk chair and linked his hands behind his neck. "What evidence do you have to prove that statement?"

"Easy. Besides tinkering on your inventions in the workroom, the applications are the only other task that consumes your attention, so you forget to eat and don't notice when it's quitting time." She pointed to the atomic clock on the wall. Last year's Christmas gift from Mallory, the device additionally displayed the current moon phase, temperature, humidity, wind chill, wind speed, wind direction, UV index, barometric pressure, rainfall, and dew point.

He huffed. "Tinkering?"

"A scientific term." She straightened the frames on the wall. "How's this application coming?"

"Well…" He considered how much she would want to hear and how much he should try to explain.

She peered over his shoulder at the computer screen. "I see

you've drafted the claims. And the drawings have your handwritten reference numbers on them." She straightened. "So, it's time for you to dictate the specification."

He glanced at her with surprise. She had picked up the process quickly. "Right you are. As soon as I complete more research into the prior art, I will spew techno-words into this apparatus for your listening and typing enjoyment tomorrow morning."

"Techno prosaic with an ly here and an ing there. For these applications, you make up language by attaching suffixes to harmless words."

"Patentese." Marc rubbed his eyes. "Or do you prefer I use some of that country lyric lingo of Chuck Daniels's you listen to?"

"That's Charlie Daniels." She clucked her tongue at his faux pas. "It wouldn't hurt for you to broaden your cultural horizons to music that includes words." She collected his empty mug and was whistling *Devil Went Down To Georgia* when she stopped at the doorway. "See you tomorrowly morningly."

He heard the front door close and knew she had gone for the day. Unfolding from his computer-focused slouch, Marc stood and took a deep breath. The scent of lavender lingered. Checking the time and outdoor temperature recorded on the atomic clock, he wondered what music Violet would listen to on her way to wherever she would go after work. Did she sing in the car?

He twisted his back until it cracked and returned his attention to his prior art research for the Meissner Device application. For the final aspect in the process, he activated the recorder and began the long and laborious task of dictation.

"The prior art indicates that there has been interest in gravity control propulsion research with such terms as antigravity, anti-gravitation, barycentric, counterbary, electrogravitics or eGrav, gravitics, G-projects, gravity control, and gravity propulsion, being used in the literature. Such approaches have dealt with the attempted manipulation of gravity or the production of gravity-like fields for propulsion."

He flipped pages on his legal pad to find a set of notes and followed the smell of coffee to the small kitchen. Violet had set a pot to brew before she left. He carried the pot and a clean cup back to his desk. Since Violet had begun working, his used and stained cups that had formerly grown into biohazards, appeared miraculously clean and shelved in the kitchenette. "Several universities have done basic research into the nature of gravity and how it interacts with electromagnetic fields. The present invention, in contrast to these attempts to block or manipulate gravity, uses the projection of a magnetic field exclusionary barrier or boundary through which an external magnetic field does not extend."

Reaching for a magnet from the stack on his desk, he held it in mid-air. Passing a pencil around the magnet, he described the process into the recorder. "The exclusionary boundary encompasses a three-dimensional space defined by the boundary projected from the Meissner Device from within the boundary itself. While the present invention is not truly the exclusion of magnetic fields due to superconductivity, as is the case in the Meissner effect, it is convenient to refer to this as a Meissner device."

Dropping the pencil, Marc balanced the magnet across his index finger. "The Meissner Device projects this exclusionary boundary which then allows the device to float in the ambient magnetic fields. Similar, for example, to a submarine that is submerged. The submarine has its own exclusionary boundary, which is the hull of the boat. The controlled volume of air and water contained in the ballast tanks provides buoyancy. The Meissner Device becomes buoyant in a sea of magnetic fields. Someone describe more fully herein this device along with methods of controlling the buoyancy and the propulsion control."

Hours of dictation fueled by caffeine, culminated in a digital dictation file that he left on Violet's desk. Right next to her oft-played recording of Charlie Daniels.

Chapter Sixteen

Tim had something for the blackmailer. A foreign agent, no doubt. Judging from his skin tones and speech, Tim guessed the man was Asian or from India, though he didn't know what corporation, knowledge broker, or government the stolen information would be pedaled to.

Did the beetle-like man, who scurried unseen in and out of deserts, countries, parking garages, Patent Office, and Tim's life represent a single government? Or did he twist products from spineless cowards like Tim and market them to the highest bidder in some clandestine auction?

Tim had followed the instructions, delivered the data, and now breathed a deep sigh of relief. Not exactly the prizewinner of inventions, but the patent had been subject to a secrecy order. Tim had played small in this espionage game, like he did in life, and hoped the effort would satisfy the blackmailer or at least prove that Tim would not be worth his time. Either way, the man who reminded him of a cockroach would surely go away.

At home that evening, Tim wrinkled his nose when he entered his apartment. No doubt he'd been so distracted over these past weeks that leftovers in the refrigerator had expired. Tim longed to return to his dull, lonely evenings wallowing in self-pity. He went to the bathroom to check his sugar and administer his customary injection. Swinging open the medicine chest, he glimpsed an image reflected in the mirrored door. Slowly, he swung the vanity mirror back several inches until he saw what had caught his eye. Something lay in the bathtub.

Leaving the mirror to swing, he cautiously approached the white porcelain tub. The source of the putrid smell. His neighbor's cat, their beloved pet. Now a ghastly, grisly sight. Horror and fear flooded into his throat, and he quickly leaned over the toilet and retched.

Sweaty and trembling, Tim fled from his apartment and into the cool night air. Directionless, he ran past restaurants whose dinner aromas caused his stomach to knot, dodged pedestrians, and threaded through yellow taxis gleaming under streetlights while waiting for their next fare. He ran until he couldn't run anymore. Breathless, he bent and rested his hands on his knees. Guttural moans gurgled in his throat. Straightening, he gulped in great amounts of air. His heart thudded against his ribcage, drowning out the bass music that spilled from a nearby bar and pounded from passing car radios.

He walked, passing familiar streets crowded with businesses. He wandered neighborhoods whose streets were alight with bobbing headlights from passing cars. He thought about never going back. Not to his address. Not to his neighbors who would ask if he had seen their missing kitty. Not to work. Surviving by his wits would surely be easier than facing what loomed back there, waiting for him. Not just the corpse of a beloved pet, but the insidious demands of a blackmailer that would never be satisfied. Would always want more. Threatening him. Demanding he do, and be, what he couldn't and wasn't. He raked a hand through his hair and cursed.

Collapsing onto a park bench, he put his head in his hands and sobbed. Huge, shuddering sobs. When he'd cried himself dry, Tim lay on his back on the bench. Staring at the stars, he recognized the physical signs of shock. And knew he needed that injection. How easy to simply deny himself the insulin and disappear into a diabetic coma.

A coward's escape, he admitted. Far from bold like his passionate wife, he had lived in fear for so long that being a coward remained the single practiced skill he did well.

Above, the moon shone clear in the night sky, trailed by the little star that dogs behind. When his son turned three, father and son had watched a lunar eclipse. In their short time together, he formed memories like snapshots that Tim occasionally pulled from the library of his mind and viewed through the lens of time.

Thoughts of his son brought him back to the present. He pushed himself into a sitting position and filtered options through his training as an engineer. If he didn't go back, they would destroy his son. That stark message had been left in the bathtub. Though Tim contemplated ending his own life, this wasn't about him. He had already abandoned his son to the currents of politics and culture. No. He could not fail his son again. Though this decision could be his last, this time Tim would protect his son.

Reluctantly, his legs feeling equal parts concrete and quivering Jell-O, he set out for what awaited him at home.

Chapter Seventeen

"Though still in a theoretical stage, the Meissner Field Generator has unlimited potential for frictionless transportation of everything from people to cargo. Even for planetary exploration." Marc stood at the front of an Advanced Physics class. From the rows of chairs in the lecture hall, 150 Indiana University students stared at him.

"Sounds like a magician's trick," smirked a boy, slouching in his seat. The girl next to him slapped him on the top of his head.

"Levitated above the ground," Marc picked up a notebook from the closest student's desk and balanced the book on his fingertips, "this system would essentially eliminate the static and dynamic friction the engines in our vehicles primarily are used to overcome."

"How will it improve the environment?" A girl with blonde braids wanted to know.

"If perfected, Meissner Field Generators would be an environmentally clean system and use miniscule amounts of energy." Marc returned the notebook to its owner, who asked, "What are the economic ramifications?"

"With the cost of fuel these days," Marc pulled his wallet from his back pocket as the visual aid, "this will prove a dynamic boost to the economy presently stressed under high fuel costs. Not only will consumers have more money in their pocket, but consider the jobs created to retool our infrastructure."

The slouching boy slouched further in his seat and rested his sandaled feet on the back of the chair in front of him. "Aren't you considered a crackpot inventor?"

Several students snickered. From his seat in the front row, the professor jumped up and faced his class. "Mr. Wayne, like many great inventors, is viewed by some as eccentric. But I assure you, his work is well-respected, and he is a frequently invited guest lecturer at universities and scientific conferences."

Tucking his wallet back into his jeans, Marc leaned on the lecture stand. "Thank you, Professor, but for a serious inventor, being called a crackpot merely proves he's in the game."

A geeky-looking guy in the back gave Marc a thumbs up.

The professor pushed up his glasses and sat.

"Nikola Tesla." Marc watched the crowd for signs of recognition. Several students nodded their heads. "The Austrian inventor who became an American citizen in 1891, is best known for many revolutionary contributions in the field of electricity and magnetism in the late nineteenth and early twentieth centuries. But due to his eccentric personality, seemingly unbelievable and sometimes bizarre claims about possible scientific and technological developments, Tesla was ostracized and regarded as a mad scientist."

Along one wall of the classroom were poster-sized photos. Marc pointed to a portrait next to a familiar image of Orville and Wilbur Wright's maiden flight. "Indiana's own Art Smith was called the Smash-Up Kid. At his home in Fort Wayne, Smith studied books and articles about flight. He believed he could improve on the Wright brothers' design. His parents believed in Smith and provided him with nearly $2,000—"

Someone gave a low whistle.

Marc nodded. "For a business investment, that's small change today. But in 1910, that was a lot of money. His invention reached nearly 50 miles per hour, rose alarmingly, dipped, rose again, and crashed."

"Ouch," came a voice from the back.

"Indeed. Art was thrown onto the frozen ground and severely injured." Marc crossed the room and stood next to Art Smith's picture. "On October 11, 1911, he flew from Fort Wayne to the nearby city of New Haven. That earned him the new nickname, Bird Boy. He went on to become a world-class showman and celebrity, known for dazzling crowds with his daring flying."

Marc shoved his hands into his pants pockets. "Any questions for this crackpot?"

The students laughed, and Marc pointed to a young man with his hand raised.

"Like," the student cleared his throat, "how would such an invention benefit our military?"

"The way I see it, there could be significant reductions in the cost and bulk of a weapon delivery system. Presently," he returned to the front of the room as he spoke, "how much of a missile does what the missile is designed to do?"

The student who had asked the question answered. "A warhead on a missile is only a small fraction of the total mass."

"Exactly." Marc nodded. "Why?"

"Well," the student considered. "A significant amount of fuel is required to move the weight of the warhead to its intended target."

"So," Marc used a marker to draw the outline of a missile on the dry erase board at the front of the lecture hall. "This much of the system is warhead, and this larger section is the support system necessary to deliver the weapon to target. What is the consequence of the design?"

The geeky-looking guy in the back folded his arms and spoke confidently. "Weight places constraints on the ability of the missile to avoid countermeasures such as an anti-missile missile."

Marc drew an arrow to the fuel section. "The largest investment for a typical intercontinental ballistic missile is in the delivery system. By developing and employing the Meissner Field Generator, heavy cargo can be transported for a fraction of the cost."

A girl shrugged off the arm the boy with flip-flops had draped around her shoulders. "All this talk of war and blowing things up is so typically male." She fingered her earring. "What are the peaceful applications for this device?"

"Harnessing the Meissner Effect would change the way we transport everything," Marc answered. "Heavy construction materials will be moved effortlessly. Our roads will look like a Disneyland ride as vehicles hover above the ground."

"With transportation hovering above ground, will we need roads or just landing terminals," she wanted to know.

Marc replaced the marker into the white board tray. "That's probably the best part. Using the Meissner Field, we make roads obsolete."

She rolled her eyes. "Sounds like a rerun of the television show *Jetsons*."

"Like Luke Skywalker's Land Speeder in the classic Star Wars films." The redheaded student in the back demonstrated by circling his hand, held flat, in the air.

"Quite," Marc agreed. "Even better, land once monopolized for asphalt roads can be used for farming, recreation, and living areas."

The girl who had asked about environmental benefits leaned forward. "All that agricultural land could end world hunger."

"With respect to the females in our class," the boy who had asked about military benefits gave a mock bow to the girl who had asked about peaceful applications, "how can we use this to gain a military edge?"

"Back to missiles." Marc returned to the lectern. "The greatest benefit lies in the ability to be undetected. The Achilles heel of the intercontinental missile is its limited steering capacity.

Like anything predictable, the weapon is easy to intercept."

Marc pressed a button on his laptop, and an image appeared on the overhead screen. The video showed the launch of an interceptor missile. The narrative described, "The present system is a method of interception. When an Intercontinental Ballistic Missile is detected by a satellite, an anti-missile missile can be launched to intercept the ICBM."

On the screen, the darkness of near-earth space exploded into vibrant flames as an interceptor missile cleanly connected with an intercontinental missile safely above the earth.

The short video ended, and Marc explained. "In contrast to current weapons like the ICBM, a weapon delivery system powered by a Meissner Field Generator could theoretically fly at low altitude, just above the ocean waves, and under the radar. Such a device could be programmed to follow an unpredictable path, or simply join the stream of commerce."

The students in the lecture hall sat silent, taking in the significant ramifications of a weapon that navigated outside the realm of predictability.

After a quiet pause, the geek in the back shifted. "That makes the nation who develops the Meissner Field Device nearly invincible."

Chapter Eighteen

Massaging his temples, Tim once more scanned the troublesome patent application. Like a pinball that ricocheted from obstacle to obstacle, his thoughts bounced from the blackmailer to his work. He wasn't making much progress with either.

He didn't want to betray his integrity and his job by forwarding sensitive military information. He'd experienced cultures in conflict. Globally, tensions erupted into war, killing, and hideous rebar-reinforced walls. Literal walls like the one in Israel. Figurative walls like the one between himself and his small family that were harder to breach than concrete ones. Personally, conflict caused him to see himself for the spineless coward he was, living alone and hollowly pining for his wife and son. For family. For community. For relationship.

He didn't want to, couldn't, be a catalyst for more of the same. His eyes went back to the patent application he had been considering for days. Without doubt, this required top secret status. Such a fantastic device would revolutionize the world. A few innovations had done just that—submarines, missiles, the Internet. Of course, the military would be the first to develop and use this. The country that implemented this transportation system would be—Tim rubbed his temples again—that country would be militarily superior. A world power. Invincible.

Rocking back in his office chair, Tim weighed his options. The United States had a reputation backed by a long history for aiding nations worldwide. Unlike other conquerors, Americans didn't appropriate the cultures they helped or defeated. He thought again of the Arabs who held Bethlehem and the Temple Mount and still bombed innocent children in Jerusalem schools.

Though his superior frowned on the practice, Tim hit the print button. He couldn't remember the last time he had looked at an application on hard copy. All reviews were conducted over the computer screen. The practice proved simpler and more secure that way. But today Tim made an exception, partly because he was having difficulty focusing and partly because he hoped if he spread the entire project in front of him, he would be able to put his finger on what kept him from forwarding this to the next step in the process.

Chapter Nineteen

Morning dawned in the red-light district near the United States capitol. Mr. Spencer had been awake for hours, plotting, while the Asian half-breed he had spent the night with slept curled at his side. He watched as she stirred and stretched, much like a cat waking from a nap. Rolling over, she smiled and traced his chest with a lacquered fingertip.

"You like, Mr. Spencer?"

He caught her wrist in a vice-like grip and fear instantly replaced her smile. "Last night I liked very much. Now I like some breakfast."

He released her, and she scrambled from the bed, tossed a housecoat over her slender frame, and scurried from the room. Lying back, he laced his fingers behind his head and stared up at the ceiling. In moments, the satisfying aroma of sizzling butter made his stomach growl.

Soon she returned with two plates. Piled high on the dish she handed to him were eggs and bright chorizo, spicy kimchi, and white toast. He devoured the hot breakfast and two cups of coffee while she observed him over her own serving of toast and fruit.

Typical for the neighborhood, he heard the sounds of others in the nearby apartments. Dogs barked, a child cried, and the whine of bad water pipes told him someone in the unit upstairs took a shower. With his belly full, he showered, dressed, and went outside.

Mist colored the outdoors a ghostly gray. Near his car,

Spencer glanced back and spied a boy about seven, his gaze hard and unblinking. Spencer continued on his way for several more paces before he looked back. Sure enough, from the shadows, the boy still watched.

Anger surged through the man. Accustomed to spying on others, he did not like being observed. He climbed into his rental car, drove around the corner, and parked. Spencer stealthily made his way back to the apartment complex but found the shadowy area vacant. Retracing his steps from the night before, he saw movement going into the address where he had spent the night.

Slipping silently inside the door, he heard the water running behind the closed door of the bathroom and knew the girl stood in the shower. From the kitchen came the sound of a dish scraping against the table. Drawing his knife, Spencer peered around the corner into the room.

Chapter Twenty

The tactical room sounded noisy as employees from different departments gathered. Tangy colognes vied with strong perfumes. Most were dressed in business blue.

"Stuffed shirts all wearing the same hairstyle and trying to run or ruin the country." Mallory took a tall backed chair next to Thomas.

He raised an eyebrow. "Pretty cynical, considering we represent that."

"Speak for yourself."

Conversations regarding football and NASCAR quieted when Deverell burst into the room, speaking before he sat down. "Talk to me, people. How is Red Riding Hood leaking information out of the United States Patent Office?"

Resembling an out of shape linebacker, a portly man spoke. "We're monitoring the phones."

"Grandma, what big ears you have." Deverell pulled a pen from behind his ear and pointed in the man's direction. "What about cell phones?"

"Not allowed in the workplace, sir, and we're listening for anyone who found a way to get one inside."

Deverell turned to a woman with bleached blonde hair. "My department," she reported, "is watching for potential methods employees might use to smuggle applications out of the building."

"Grandma, what big hands you have." Deverell tapped the pen on the tabletop. "How is the wolf gaining entry to Granny's house and cherry picking from the cookie jar?"

"Patent applications are submitted by express mail or through the Internet." Mallory held up a printout of a patent application. "They are processed on the computer. By hitting a few keystrokes, an application could be diverted to a new destination."

"Grandma, what big eyes you have." Deverell swiveled his chair to the left. "Jimmy?"

Brown eyes behind John Lennon spectacles, Jimmy drummed long fingers against a mug of green chai tea. "Computer forensics is already on it."

"And?"

"And we are in the fun stage. Looking. Searching. Exploring. Considering the options and possibilities."

Across the table, the portly man gave a snort. "That's code for doesn't have a clue."

With a middle finger, Jimmy exaggeratedly pushed his glasses on his nose. "Translation courtesy of the auditory department's ass...," he took a drink from the cup, "sets."

Several people snickered.

Deverell ignored the slight. "Where is our patent application for the Meissner Device in the process now?"

Mallory spoke up, pleased that her plan progressed precisely as she had calculated. This may be her first time as the lead on a project, yet the strategy had come together swimmingly. She shoved down a feeling of pride. She considered herself made for this type of leadership, a natural. "The application is exactly where we wanted it to be—being examined for a secrecy order."

Chapter Twenty-one

Following a lively question and answer session, Marc collected his computer he had used to show the film clip and slid the laptop into a carrying case. From the lectern at the front of the classroom where Marc had given his guest presentation, the professor assigned homework and dismissed the class.

"As always, thanks for coming, Marc." The professor walked with him to the door.

"The students are refreshing. Their quick wit and probing questions keep me from getting stale in my dusty office and cluttered lab."

The older man ran a hand through his unruly gray hair. "Each year students seem less refined, no respect anymore for social graces and protocol."

"They probably slurp designer coffee drinks in comfortable clothes and talk about us dinosaurs." Marc clapped the weary professor on the shoulder. "Be good to them. They will design your old age living conditions."

Tossing the professor a goodbye salute, Marc walked toward the parking lot. Preparing for the Little 500, a string of collegiate guys and girls pedaled past on bicycles. The clusters of bicyclists around campus resembled the flocks of Canadian geese taking to the skies in their yearly migration to winter in warmer climates. Retired Indiana residents, affectionately called snowbirds, followed the geese to Florida for the cold months and returned in the spring to resume their volunteer work at the library and hospital. While Indiana residents didn't always know their way around the Hoosier state, they had long considered Florida to be a suburb.

In the spirit of the historic Indy 500 in nearby Indianapolis, the Little 500 remained a popular attraction on campus and a favorite in the surrounding community. The largest collegiate bike race in the nation, the yearly intramural event drew crowds numbering 25,000 to watch the four-person teams compete around a quarter-mile track. Proceeds funded working student scholarships. The final year Marc had participated as a student, riders in the one-day event collected $40,000.

For the majority of bicyclists, the Little 500 became their first competition. Marc had agreed to make a three-some into a four-some after he had been the recipient of Little 500 monies. Ribbing from the other three who accused him of being parked so frequently in the lab that he suffered from vitamin D deficiency, helped his decision to get involved.

"Been an addiction ever since," Marc said to himself.

"Can I carry that for you?"

The voice came from behind. Without waiting for an answer, a wiry student with red hair came alongside and reached for Marc's weighty computer bag. He eagerly stuck out his right hand. "Interesting presentation in class, Mr. Wayne."

Marc accepted the firm handshake, noting the boy's *Li'l Abner* t-shirt. "Chivalry is not completely dead."

"Excuse me?"

"Never mind." Marc squinted at him. "You're the guy in the back of the room." Marc declined to add the geeky-looking guy in the back of the room.

"Aspiring crackpot." The student eagerly fell into step next to Marc. "I'd like to show you something I've been working on."

Marc glanced at his watch.

"It won't take long." The words tumbled out, picking up

speed. "And I can talk fast."

"Just calculating." Marc nodded to his watch. "When I was a student, I ate every two hours. You and I just came from a three-hour class, and I'm hungry."

The young man grinned. "I can show you where they serve the biggest and best burgers."

"Lead on, Kimosabe."

"Hebron, actually. Hebron Heath." He shifted his backpack to balance the load with the weight of Marc's computer.

Another four-some on bikes pedaled past, the last guy calling encouragement like a goose at the back of a flying vee.

Marc glanced at his new companion. "Do you ride in the Little 500?"

His shoulder drooping with the weight of Marc's bag, Hebron looked sidelong at him. "Do I look like the athletic type?"

"An inventor invented the bicycle."

"And inventors have been modifying the design ever since." Hebron pointed to his oversized feet. "And athletic shoes. Job security."

"Even inventors ride bikes. I'm the visual aid."

Hebron shook his head. "I prefer mental workouts."

"Same argument I used."

"Huh?"

"Get on a bike. Your body will enjoy the attention and your mind will solve problems in the fresh air. Besides," Marc looked him up and down. "You could use some sun."

Hebron held out his pale arms, Marc's computer bag hanging from his left hand like a ripe fig on a tree. "Do I look like I tan?"

Chapter Twenty-two

Something niggled at Tim about the patent application.

He'd kept the submission at his desk longer than any other project. Would something this significant satisfy the blackmailer enough that he would leave Tim alone? Such a unique design, should there be an investigation, would surely be traced back to his desk. Worse, Tim felt terrified to unleash such technology into the wrong hands. The man in the parking garage who demanded secrets surely sought to empower an ambitious leader.

Tim spread the troublesome application on his desk, studied the design until the figures blurred and the words no longer made sense. Then, once more, he set the papers aside. From his desk drawer, he retrieved a bottle of pain medication. He shook two tablets into his palm, considered the size and intensity of his headache, and shook out two more. From the same drawer, he added two stomach lozenges. With a mug of yesterday's cold coffee, he downed the tablets. Rolling the lozenges around in his mouth, he stood and began to pace.

In 2005, the USPTO issued US Patent 6,960,975 to Boris Volfson of Huntington, Indiana, for his design of an antigravity space vehicle. Designs for perpetual motion machines had been submitted since the turn of the twentieth century. Patent applications on such devices became so numerous that by 1911, the patent office ruled that perpetual motion machine concepts had to be accompanied by a model that could run in the office for a period of one year. The rule was later dropped.

Theoretically powered by a superconductor shield that changed the space-time continuum in such a way to defy gravity, Volfson's patent made the news. Physicists claimed the design was impossible. The USPTO's official response noted that mistakes were inevitable. With 5,000 examiners handling a workload of 350,000 applications yearly, patents may be granted to unworkable ideas.

Tim's need to keep his name out of the headlines loomed as strong as the pressure on him to provide something to the blackmailer. But he didn't dare risk playing small again. He thought of the neighbor's pet.

And his son.

The penalty extracted by the blackmailer struck too dear. Cost too much.

"Hi, Tim."

Startled, Tim stopped pacing and stared at the intruder.

"I brought you something." She came forward and put a cup in his hands. "Fresh brewed." She wore a form fitting black skirt and a bright shirt with a deep V-neck.

"Oh, uh, thank you." *What was her name? The Hispanic woman who had walked with him to the atrium?* He still couldn't remember.

"Are you all right?" She came closer and held his gaze with her brown eyes.

How did she get in this secured section of the building?

Tim shrugged. "Fine."

She tilted her head flirtatiously. "Do you always pace in your office?" She glided to his desk and picked up the irksome application.

"I don't think you're cleared—"

"Of course. I was just curious about what was troubling you." She replaced the project on his desk. "Can I help?"

Tim gazed into her upturned face. Slowly, he shook his head.

"No, I don't believe so."

"But you are worried."

He blinked and stepped back. "No, no, I'm fine."

She tapped his coffee cup with a red fingernail. "Well, drink your coffee while it's still hot." She spun on a stiletto heel and left, her heels echoing down the hallway.

Had he been so lost in thought that he hadn't heard her approach? Or had she come in more quietly than she left? He shook his head to clear the questions. He felt suspicious of everyone lately. Best get this blackmailer off his back once and for all.

Dropping into his chair, he picked up the application again. What bothered him about this piece? He went over the USPTO criteria. Was the idea patentable by law? Was the design new? Based on the current state of science, did the application describe the idea in a manner to enable someone skilled in that technology to make and use the design? Taking a long drink of his coffee, Tim began his review back at the top.

Moments later, he sprang to his feet. Of course. The application appeared complete, but now Tim realized a section of the information was theoretical. Theory. But not functional. That's what had rankled him like a blackberry seed in his wisdom tooth. A vital aspect had not been included. From a patent perspective, the proposal was non-enabling. Someone skilled in the art of this technology would be prevented from building this device.

Under ordinary circumstances, Tim would have rejected the application and sent a notice of the fact to the inventor. He checked the applicant's name again. Marc Wayne. A legitimate inventor and patent attorney.

For the first time in weeks, Tim smiled. He laughed. How perfect. He'd give this patent application to the creep. This would satisfy the blackmailer's demand for something important. The design appeared complete. Tim doubted anyone but he would recognize the problem, and even he had taken a long time to spot the irregularity though this fell within his specialization.

Tim could trick the beetle man and send the hostile government on a pointless chase of time, manpower, and money. Ironic justice. Anyone who stooped to such devious methods deserved to be outwitted.

Confident he held the answer to his dilemma, he squelched an urge to whoop with relief. This Meissner Effect Generator seemed too good to be true. Because it was.

Chapter Twenty-three

Spencer spied the urchin in the kitchen. With both hands, the boy hungrily stuffed cold leftover eggs and toast into his mouth.

"You little…"

At the sound of Spencer's voice, the boy looked up, his mouth agape and crammed with chewed scrambled eggs. His eyes widened at the sight of the knife in the man's hand, and he dropped the toast that was halfway to his mouth.

Spencer lunged, grabbing for the small intruder.

Pulling the table between them, the boy ran. In a powerful thrust, Spencer shoved the table to the far side of the room where the cheap piece of furniture crashed against the wall, scattering eggs and broken dishes. He launched himself at the screaming boy, and man and child tumbled into the living room.

Quickly, Spencer pinned the boy. "What are you doing sneaking around…"

The boy spit and bit and kicked and attempted to scratch. Spencer had his hands full trying to subdue the wild child. Suddenly, from behind, a wet towel covered his face, pressing heavily upon his nose and mouth, suffocating him. Panicked, Spencer staggered to his feet. Tugging at the weight clinging to his neck and head, he crashed blindly against furniture and walls until he shook loose. He pulled the towel from his head and sucked in large gulps of air. Turning, he saw the girl, naked and bruised, in a heap against the wall. The towel that she had held over his head he dropped over her.

Whirling, he searched the room for the boy. The front door stood open, and the kid had disappeared. Spencer went outside and searched for signs indicating which direction his young prey had dashed. But the landscape didn't lend a clue. The street rat proved adept at disappearing into his own territory.

Back inside, he heard the girl moan. Where she rubbed her head, a lump rapidly formed.

"The thief was stealing—"

She began to shake her head and quickly stopped. "Not a thief." She pressed her palms to her forehead. "My son."

He cursed.

"You go." She spoke the words softly.

He went to the kitchen. Crunching over broken glass from the broken dishes, he reached into the freezer and pulled out a package of snow peas. Returning to the living room, he found the woman had moved to the couch.

He handed her the frozen bag of vegetables. "Put this on your head."

She did as he instructed, though she refused to meet his eyes. "His father?"

She gave a slight shrug. "No father."

He went to the window and gazed out at the eerie shadows exaggerated by the lingering fog. Somewhere out there hid the hungry, fatherless son of a prostitute. Street smart, emotionally undeveloped with hyper-developed survival instincts, he lived in the moment. Without a conscience, he survived as a high risk-taker.

Spencer had been that kid on the other side of the world. Begging from tourists and picking their pockets to survive, the cruel lifestyle had been characterized by beatings from adults who caught him stealing and beatings from bigger street kids who stole from him what he had stolen.

Ill-fed and small anyway, as a teen, Spencer passed himself

off as a younger child when the claim served him. Unwanted and uninvited, the memory he had long ago buried now surfaced like an infected boil. He cursed again. The toxic remembrance would have to be lanced and purged. In the past, he had tried alcohol and drugs. Not even sex restored his ego from the sudden revisit to his former humiliation. To secure his hard-won state of control and power, the demons of his past had to be exorcized.

But who? He took stock of his business. His former information supplier in the patent office had been a willing puppet. Spencer's exchange of money with the employee had been a simple transaction. Give Spencer something he could sell for a great deal of money, and Spencer would deposit an admirable sum into the marionette's bank account. But the arrangement went awry. Financially secure, the employee retired unannounced and early. Spencer found himself holding clipped strings with no one to dance at the other end.

Never one to repeat a mistake, Spencer employed blackmail to motivate a new player. A terrified weakling, the mark resembled a sweating stick of dynamite. Spencer's life depended on keen judgment of character. Like a ticking bomb, he knew that eventually this arrangement would backfire, and he had no intention of getting caught in the explosion. Diffusing the problem quickly became necessary on a business level. Now he must take action on a personal level.

Without a glance at the discarded girl, he strode purposefully into the gray morning.

Chapter Twenty-four

True to his word, Hebron led Marc to a hamburger diner that promised breakfast all day. Dropping onto chrome stools with red vinyl seats, the two bellied up to the bar and gave their order to the waitress. From their ringside spots, those at the counter could watch the food fry on a grill the size of a flight deck.

The cook slathered the hot grill with margarine. Like a symphony conductor, the white-aproned expert threw eggs and hash browns to sizzle, adding ladles of melt-in-your-mouth flapjack batter to the crackling, popping breakfast serenade. Next, he plopped quarter-pound burger patties on top of thick slices of bacon for the bacon burgers the two had ordered. Round slabs of provolone cheese topped the burger patties. The aroma smelled heavenly, and Marc's stomach growled.

In short order, the short order cook had medium rare patties on oversized buns, accompanied by a generous side of potato salad dished from a large plastic tub in the wall-sized refrigerator. The special included frosty glasses of fresh lemonade and a foot long dill pickle.

"I could pack on the freshman fifteen here." Marc took a large bite of his burger, letting the hot cheese stick to the roof of his mouth.

As if strumming guitar strings, Hebron ran his fingers over his ribs. "Hasn't had that effect on me yet, but I keep giving it another try."

"Very sportsmanlike."

Marc had only eaten half his burger when Hebron finished his platter-sized meal. "You got a tapeworm?"

"How old are you?"

"Touché."

The student pushed back his plate. "Now for my invention."

From his jeans pocket, Hebron pulled three guitar picks, a tuning fork, and a harmonica. Frowning, he fished in his other pocket and retrieved a collection of wires and conductors.

Marc watched his lunch companion pull objects from pockets like a magician finding doves in a hat. "You lost it?"

"Nah, I always have it with me. Somewhere." Reaching into his backpack, he continued his search until his eyes lit up. "Found it."

Seeing the hardware store appear on the counter, the waitress removed their plates, stacking them loudly. Marc snatched the dill pickle before she could whisk away the condiment with the burger drippings.

Hebron proudly set his creation on the counter between them. The size of a dessert dish, the device resembled a softball stitched together with scraps of lightweight metal. Using a wire clasp from his pocket collection, the inventor opened the sphere to reveal layers and a hollow interior.

He looked expectantly at Marc. "Whatcha think?"

"May I?" Marc wiped pickle juice on his napkin and reached for the unusual object. Holding the sphere one way and then another, he inspected the design and materials.

"Well?"

"Tell me about it."

The young man's expression fell. "You can't tell what it does?"

"On the contrary, Hebron. It appears to measure—"

"Precisely! Cut, clarity, and color."

The waitress refilled Marc's glass. "Talking about my best

friends?"

Marc looked up. "Diamonds?"

She smiled. "Of course."

"See, Hebron. Even the waitress knows what you're working on."

Hebron glanced up at the collegiate pouring lemonade from the cold pitcher. The girl winked and moved away to seat a loud group of students who had just entered. Marc recognized the bikers he had seen earlier pedaling around campus and knew they would be hungry after their strenuous exercise.

Marc elbowed Hebron. "Focus."

The boy flushed and tore his attention from the pretty waitress. "The receptors analyze a stone for color and clarity." From the depths of his backpack, he pulled a small stone and handed it to Marc. "The device produces a three-dimensional enlargement to show inconsistencies in the organic makeup or man-made cut."

"The diamond industry spends a half-million dollars for devices that do what you say this one does." Marc placed the stone inside. "You've tested it?"

Hebron raised his voice to talk above the boisterous newcomers. "Works as smooth as the bike you're trying to get me to ride."

"What do you measure with?"

Hebron pulled the straw from his lemonade to use as a pointer. "The acoustical membrane, when activated, causes light to be reflected. The membrane circles the subject. The receptor analyzes the diamond based on the light received."

Marc nodded. "A light CAT scan."

"A poor man's CAT scan for diamonds."

Chapter Twenty-five

Tim's fingers trembled as he typed on the computer keyboard. He felt caught in what the Americans termed a Catch-22. If he got caught, he would be prosecuted as a spy against the United States. If he didn't do this, he had no doubt that the threats of the sinister man to take the life of his son would be carried out.

Sweat beaded on his forehead. In a last, though laughably feeble act of defiance, he altered the steganography algorithm of a photo of a cat to carry the information he traded for the life of his son. Though assured that this redistribution of the photos' pixel information could not be detected, he remained skeptical. In his line of work, Tim knew that for every innovative encryption, another innovative mind developed a cipher.

Secrets upon secrets had burdened Tim. Mere months ago, he considered what he did today to be unthinkable. Brushing the moisture from his face, Tim studied the screen a final time. Then, with a single ridiculously simple movement of a single finger, he quickly tapped the send key, transmitting the seemingly innocent photo of a cuddly kitten.

The deed done, he fell back in his office chair. The top secret patent information for the Meissner Effect Device had been delivered to the inbox of the foul and brutal man with the swift knife.

Chapter Twenty-six

Yao felt optimistic about the current project.

Gritting back his memories once more, the Colonel arrived at the prototype lab. His military superiors, including General Gao, had provided the facility, the scientists, and a short time frame for Yao to develop something to give China military superiority. They expected results. Quickly.

The modern technology in the lab reflected a stark contrast to the ancient building that housed the hopes for his country's rise to an uncontested world power. Yao had suggested they monitor the United States Patent and Trademark Office for cutting-edge innovations.

America had enjoyed her position as the superior world power since her victory in World War II. After his time in the United States, Yao understood that the land of the free allowed—even encouraged—freedom of thought. This freedom produced prosperity through capitalism. Well-fed and uncensored thinkers created technology that paved the way for their continued advancement.

As the most efficient means to accomplish his end, Yao harvested the next great inventions while the United States bound up the ideas in processes and paperwork spurred by expanding federal government control. While the patent office became increasingly anchored in methodical procedures, unfettered by burdensome bureaucracy, Yao would develop the invention.

That's where the man known as Mr. Spencer had come in. He

knew how to get what Yao wanted. And what Spencer siphoned from the patent office met the expectations the Colonel had hoped for. The development of the new jet engine that gave his country superior mobility in the skies had been Yao's first victory. He dared be ambitious for more.

Historically, Yao considered the United States slow to realize the value of flight for military superiority. Three years after the Wright brothers flew the world's first powered flight at Kitty Hawk in North Carolina, the Army Signal Corps formed an Aeronautical Division on August 1, 1907. Progressing from balloons and dirigibles, the Division accepted their first airplane from the innovative Wright brothers in 1909. A small band of intrepid flight pioneers, including Captain Benjamin D. Foulois, experimented with various aircraft to become the First Aero Squadron. During World War I, President Woodrow Wilson created the Army Air Service. Soon, more than 19,000 officers and 178,000 enlisted men piloted 11,754 American-made aircraft consisting mostly of trainers like the JN-4 Jenny.

Despite visionaries like Billy Mitchell, the US lagged behind European nations that created a separate air force. A peacetime establishment with limited funds for advancement, American flight remained a small interest. Until World War II. The last global scale war proved what air power proponents had championed for decades.

The end of the war paralyzed German and Japanese war economies. The two countries had been dominated by the quality and quantity of aircraft and airmen populating the skies. Yao conceded that air power didn't win the war by itself, but he had no doubt this weapon made possible the Allies' total victory over the Axis powers. Japan surrendered when Super Fortress bomber B-29s Enola Gay and Bockscar dropped atomic bombs on Hiroshima and Nagasaki.

Yao didn't have sympathy for Japan. That neighboring

country had imposed unparalleled cruelty on China's people. The common people like his parents. Like Yao had been while growing up. The horrors of the Nanking Massacre haunted his country. After committing some of history's worst war atrocities against the Chinese, unrestrained rape and murder, Japan played down and even denied that the crimes occurred.

While attending the western university, Yao had toured many places in the United States. At Pearl Harbor, he learned about the devastation wreaked by Japan's surprise attack. Japan's air power decimated that pivotal base in the Pacific. For a week, survivors heard the desperate tapping from sailors trapped underwater in the tangled wreckage of their ships. Futile calls for help that weakened as tortuous days passed, and the young sons of proud parents died of wounds and dehydration. Died, abandoned, and alone. In his opinion, arrogant Japan deserved the atomic bombs.

In one of the most lopsided battlefield victories in military history, the United States Air Force deployed halfway around the globe during 1991's Operation Desert Shield. Using sophisticated satellite navigation systems, the advanced F-117 Nighthawk delivered precision-guided munitions that neutralized Iraq's air defenses and command structure in a mere six weeks. Air power allowed coalition ground forces to liberate Kuwait with fewer casualties suffered than a typical week in the Vietnam conflict.

Yao harbored no animosity towards the United States. He saw them as a rich source of technology and ideas he could harvest for his own purposes. Yao's superiors had been pleased with the new jet engine. The Colonel had confidence he would be successful again. The Meissner Effect Generator would change the face of the world. Beginning with China.

Chapter Twenty-seven

Exhausted, Tim unlocked his front door. Inside his apartment, he tossed his briefcase onto the coffee table, loosened his tie, and stood staring out the large window, oblivious of the familiar view before him.

This marked the second time in his life that he felt completely and utterly out of control. Emasculated. Again. Minds far more cunning and fanatical than his own manipulated his actions. People he didn't even know created situations that escalated and swept him along like a lamb caught in a violent wadi flood.

He longed for a quiet existence, a simple and satisfying life. To do a good day's work and come home to the welcoming arms of his wife and the smiling face of his son who felt proud of his father.

He glanced down at his trembling hands. His vision blurred. From long pent-up emotion or low blood sugar? On top of his other sorrows, his body mocked him and reflected his weakness with diabetes.

After administering the insulin shot, he pulled a bottle of kefir from the refrigerator. Dropping onto the couch, he lifted the lid of the dusty olive wood box on the coffee table and pulled out the photo. Her beauty took his breath. His wife, holding the hand of their handsome young son. All Jewish people in Israel, males and females, spent a year or more in military service. They had met while she served her country. Neither her family nor his were pleased with the union when they married. A Muslim and a Jew.

Naively, he felt certain love would smooth over the political and religious conflicts between their backgrounds. They would be the beginning of peace between the two warring peoples who began as desert half brothers—Ishmael and Isaac.

And for a time, their love had been enough. They made their home in Bethlehem, a colorful mosaic of peoples and cultures who got along by exercising their wits. Lived, loved, worked, and had their son.

Until the year 2000. Never content to co-exist in peaceable compromise, Palestinian terrorists had slipped into adjacent Jerusalem numerous times with intent to destroy. This time, a bomb exploded on the playground of a Jewish school. Young children were dismembered. Killed. His Esther had raced to the scene. He knew she would, and he had followed to be with his wife.

Desperately threading her way through emergency personnel and others who came to help, she called and called for her sister. And her niece. Amid terrible dust, destruction, and panicked people, Esther saw through the blood and dropped to her knees beside the young mother cradling her still child. The teacher and the student. Esther's sister and her niece.

Lost in stunned shock, her sister didn't see anything or anyone except the beautiful little girl. As during the months when she rocked and sang while the child was once knit together in her womb, in a futile attempt, the mother murmured comforting words as she tried to put her daughter's torn body back together. Tears streaming down her face, Esther cradled the two until someone came to take away their bodies.

Notified of the horrible news, Esther's brother-in-law flew home from his work as an Israeli ambassador to South America. Reuven's deep grief simmered dark as he arranged for the funerals of his wife and daughter.

While Jewish families wailed for their terrible loss, back in

Bethlehem, the bombers celebrated with obscene hilarity. Tim had
followed the raucous noise. He wanted to see who was responsible.
Who would rejoice in the slaughter of children? He and Esther
were bridging the centuries old schism between Abraham's two
sons. Outraged, Tim approached the center of the festivities where
participants praised Allah for their victory over the infidels. What
triumph, Tim questioned, existed in decimating school children? In
killing teachers? What kind of god commanded his followers to
represent him in this way? Tight-lipped to hold back the explosive
anger roiling inside, Tim faced his brother.

That's where Esther found him. No matter how many ways
he explained to his wife that he had not been *with* his brother, but
had gone there to *confront* him, from that moment her eyes
reflected a perpetual sorrow born of unspeakable betrayal.

Tensions between the residents of Bethlehem and the
inhabitants of Jerusalem escalated until, to protect her children,
Israel erected a wall between the city of the Christian Christ's birth
and the city of His death.

"They deserve the wall, every inch of it," his wife said. And
the ghastly rebar-reinforced concrete wall divided her from him.
As hostilities increased, many Jewish people left Bethlehem. He
pleaded with his wife to stay.

But the next day, when he returned home from work, she and
their son were gone. He'd known as soon as he walked in the door,
even before he saw that her toothbrush no longer rested in the
medicine chest next to his. Her shoes and clothes weren't nestled
with his in their closet. Instead of his wife bright to embrace the
world and his son brimming with eagerness to explore, only a dark
hollowness shadowed him like a constant specter. An emptiness
filled his bed where she had once cradled against him.

As if echoing his previous pain, now a dull ache radiated
across his chest and left arm. The heartache that never went away.
Of course, he had followed her, found that she had returned to her

family community who welcomed her and their son, took them in and cared for them.

"I cannot bear that grotesque wall between us, separating you from me, separating people." He reached for her hand.

"Separating wolves from sheep, monsters from peaceful families." She pulled away.

"I'm going to the United States." His eyes pleaded for her. "I'll send for you and our son."

"Who knows but that I am here for such a time as this." She placed the palm of her hand briefly against his cheek and walked away.

True to his word, he immigrated to the United States. His letters to her went unanswered as he secured employment and a two-bedroom townhouse with a room for their son. Feeling powerless to bring his family together, he routinely sent money to provide for their needs. The empty years piled one on top of another, collecting like fallen leaves one autumn after another.

Reaching again into the box, he removed a second photo. His wife had sent the picture, taken on the day their son graduated from university.

Like a vise crushing his ribs, the physical pain in Tim's chest increased. Suddenly, breathing felt difficult. Water. He probably needed water.

He pushed himself to his feet, took two steps toward the kitchen, and pitched forward. As he fell, he saw the Bethlehem wall crumble and his young wife and small son running toward him, their faces beaming, their arms open to embrace him.

Chapter Twenty-eight

Yao anticipated the praise of his superiors. The Meissner Device promised to turn theory into world-changing reality.

Flashing his identification, the Colonel passed into the lab. Four scientists Yao recognized as the project leads bent over a table spread with blueprints. One man typed on a computer keyboard, and another studied the screen.

"Tell me of your progress." The Colonel approached the cluster gathered at the table.

The lead scientist spoke for the group. "We are experiencing difficulty."

The Colonel faced his fidgeting companion. "You have failed." Yao noted the flash of fear in the other man's eyes.

"No, no, Comrade Yao." Moisture glistening on his smooth forehead, the scientist clutched his shaking hands into fists and shoved them into the deep, square pockets of his lab coat. "It is our belief that a portion vital to the success of the construction has been left out of the information provided."

"Something is missing," Yao interpreted. Nervous men spoke in vague terms and used more words than necessary.

The man in front of him bobbed his head.

The Colonel indicated the others. "Surely your staff can figure out what is needed."

The scientist shifted his weight, swallowed, and began. "I, that is, *we* are not altogether convinced we are missing an ingredient." He pulled his trembling hands from his pockets and started to gesture but quickly hid them once more. "Our findings indicate there is something about the process that is not included."

"The process."

The scientist nodded. "It's an oversimplification, but perhaps I can offer an illustration."

"Perhaps you can."

"When I attended university, an American professor taught English. My wife became interested in American cooking, so the professor gave my wife a recipe for making yeast bread. Every attempt failed—" Realization of the word he had just spoken reflected in the scientist's eyes, and he glanced fearfully at his superior. "That is to say, she—my wife—experienced difficulty getting the anticipated results."

Aware of the speaker's apprehension, Yao stared at him. "Continue."

The man plunged on. "Finally, the American professor came to our home. She made the recipe with my wife."

"And the result?"

"Success."

Yao pondered this information for a moment. "You're asking to complete the project with the inventor."

Looking hopeful, he nodded.

"You're asking me to bring this American inventor to your kitchen."

Chapter Twenty-nine

Marc tilted the device and examined the delicate hinges. "If you can develop a more efficient manner of opening this…" He closed the object and manipulated the wire clasp. When the piece sprang open, he repeated the process.

The waitress set two plates before them. The dish in front of Marc held homemade blueberry pie. Deep-dish apple filled Hebron's plate. "We didn't order…" Marc tried to get the attention of the waitress.

The girl had eyes only for Hebron. "On the house." Then she moved down the counter, taking orders from new customers.

Hebron switched the pie plates and inhaled the blueberry slab in a record three bites.

"Why diamonds?" Marc quickly forked a bite into his mouth before the apple pie disappeared.

Hebron shrugged. "My dad deals in diamonds."

"The manufacturers of diamond grading machines claim progress in rating color and cut. But nearly everyone is working on a clarity unit. It's the final frontier of automated diamond grading." He scooped whipped cream from the top of his pie into his mouth. "No one has developed a reasonably priced machine that can distinguish between inclusions and reflections."

The young man nodded and forked half of Marc's pie into his mouth.

"Your dad must be thrilled with this."

"You'd think," Hebron mumbled around a mouthful of spiced

apples and crust.

Marc stared at the college student who eagerly stuffed the final bite of pie into his mouth. "I don't understand."

Hebron pointed his fork at his invention. "When it comes to diamond grading in the labs, the eyes still have it. Every major gem lab employs human graders to color-grade diamonds because machines are easily fooled. According to my dad," he dropped his voice two octaves, "the human eye and color-grading machines sometimes see color differently."

Marc leaned his elbows on the counter. "Surely, there are others in the industry who will look at your research."

"Dad's viewpoint is widely shared among gemologists. Lab execs and the gemologists agree the newer models are more accurate than the original Okuda Industries machines. Those were introduced over two decades ago. But they insist the machines can be fooled by a number of variables."

"Such as?"

Hebron ticked off the list on his fingers. "Highly fluorescent diamonds, brown body color, dark inclusions, or stone position."

Feeling his lunch settle, Marc adjusted the waist on his pants. "What about use in labs?"

Hebron picked up the invention and studied it. "Dad insists it can't be used in gemological labs for actual lab work."

"What about you? What do you think?"

For the first time since the hamburgers showed up in front of them, the young man's eyes lit up. "I know this works."

"But?"

The young inventor slumped. "But with the door closed to the diamond industry, it's a moot point."

"There is an old man named Thurmond who practically built my community. He says when you hit a wall, find a way around it."

A brief look of hurt flashed in his eyes before the college

student masked his expression. "Pop is more than a wall. He's a force in the industry."

Marc mulled this over. After the enthusiastic support he had received from his own dad, Marc mentally replaced that image of a father who apparently did the opposite for Hebron. He voiced another of Thurmond's mottos. "Unless the technology can be proven of value in another realm."

Sighing, Hebron sat back on his stool. "Exactly why I let you take me to lunch. Got any ideas?"

Hebron's attention suddenly riveted on something going on behind Marc. He turned to see the waitress exchange her apron for a sweater. She said something to the cook and went out the door.

Hebron bolted from his seat at the counter before Marc could stop him. "Hey! What about your invention?"

Hot on the trail, Hebron didn't appear to hear.

Marc stood. "Hebron! Your invention."

He turned, his feet pedaling backward. "No worries." He waved a hand good-naturedly. "I'll find you."

Then Hebron went outside and loped down the sidewalk. Through the large picture windows, Marc saw Hebron catch up to the waitress. She stopped and smiled at him. Then the two made their way back to campus and the classes and life that awaited them there.

Marc rolled the invention around in his palm. What other uses could this piece of brilliance be applied to?

Chapter Thirty

"Dead?" Deverell looked from Mallory to Thomas.

The single word stood out on the report. Mallory's only response when she received the news moments earlier had been, "Marc!"

Brushing past Thomas who tried to keep up with the woman on a mission, she sped down the hall. Finding Deverell in his windowless office, she delivered the news.

"The patent examiner is dead?" Deverell shrugged off his irritation at being interrupted.

"Last weekend." Mallory handed the updated file to her supervisor.

"How?" He came around his desk and perched on the corner.

"Natural causes," Thomas trailed Mallory into the office. "Probably a heart attack."

"What did the autopsy reveal?" Deverell reached for a pen and clicked it.

"There wasn't one." Mallory's words came like stilettos.

"Let's get one." The pen clicking increased.

Thomas shook his head. "He's already buried."

"So quickly?" Deverell's eyebrows shot up. "That's suspicious."

"The whole thing is suspicious." Mallory took the offending pen from her boss and dropped it into his coffee cup.

With a hand on her shoulder, Thomas steered Mallory to one of the two chairs arranged in front of Deverell's desk for visitors.

"When we looked into it, we discovered he's Muslim."

"Named Tim?"

"Hatim, actually." Feeling agitated, Mallory sat.

"Mother's parents are Muslim." Thomas dropped into the second chair. "The Muslim part explains why he was buried so quickly. Custom."

Deverell grunted and scanned the file until something caught his attention. "He has a grown son..."

Mallory grew more uncomfortable by the minute, the way she felt during the only horror movie she had ever watched. She shifted in her seat.

Deverell lowered his glasses and peered at her. "Something on your mind, Mallory?"

Goosebumps rose on her arms as if something ominous crept close in the dark. "I'm concerned about Marc."

Deverell gave the two of them that "I told you I didn't want to involve family" look. His silence spoke volumes.

"Look," Thomas pulled the pen from his boss's cup and tossed it back to Deverell, "involving Marc may not have been our brightest notion."

Mallory met Thomas's gaze as he took partial responsibility for the decision when they both knew the idea belonged completely to her. She opened her mouth to protest, but he quickly continued.

"However, he was—is—the prime profile for this situation. In light of the latest events—"

"He means Saad's untimely or timely demise." No longer able to contain her growing unease, Mallory shot out of her seat and paced.

Thomas cocked his head in her direction. "Mallory—we—are concerned about Marc's safety."

Deverell spun his coffee cup in lazy circles, ignoring the dribble that stained a path down one side and pooled at the base.

"The death of this mole—"

"Hatim Saad."

"The death of Hatim seems to be of plausible circumstances."

"Seemingly." Mallory emphasized the word, aware that her tone dripped sarcasm. "But it's too coincidental for me. Just as we trace some information leaks to him, he dies? C'mon, boss."

Deverell bounced his pen against the table. "You think these guys are smart killers?"

"I'm not underestimating them." Mallory faced her co-workers. Hands on hips, she spoke her mind. "I want protection for Marc. Immediately."

Deverell looked to Thomas, who nodded. "I agree with Mallory."

"Why?"

"Hatim may have been one of the examiners who saw Marc's patent application." Thomas spread his hands. "He would have known a secrecy order had been issued."

Their boss scanned the information about Hatim once again while Mallory paced and formulated a plan to provide protection for her brother, even if her supervisor opted not to grant her request.

At last, Deverell closed the file and dropped it on the desk. "All right, we'll arrange to keep a protective eye on our inventor."

"And patent attorney," Thomas corrected.

Getting her request emboldened Mallory. Now she wanted more. She stopped pacing and planted her palms on the broad desk. "I want to go."

Deverell sighed heavily. "Go ahead. Take a couple days. Make sure everything is secure in the Midwest. We'll decide if we need to send agents to protect your inventor based on what you find."

Before her supervisor stopped speaking, Mallory turned for the door. "Thanks, boss." Relief and anxiety warred in her mind.

Behind her, she heard Deverell address her partner.

"Thomas, search Hatim Saad's workspace, his house, his car. See if there is anything that indicates his death is a result of something other than natural causes."

Chapter Thirty-one

Feeling the plane began its swift descent, Mallory pressed her forehead against the window to view the scenery below. Farm fields stretched as far as she could see, like the patchwork quilts her mother used to make with the church ladies at their weekly quilting bee. She had one of their handmade creations on her bed back east in her upscale apartment. The Methodist women had pieced the small fabric blocks with tiny stitches as a gift when she left to pursue a career in the big city.

Creeks edged agricultural land and stands of trees where farmers and their sons, dressed in thick Carhartts against the winter cold, hunted deer in November. Large, red barns flanked newer metal pole barns that housed oversized green and yellow farm equipment.

Ahead, growing larger, were the tall city buildings of downtown Fort Wayne. Tucked in Indiana's upper east corner, Fort Wayne lay 18 miles west of the Ohio border and 50 miles south of neighboring Michigan. Second largest in the state, the city had been named for President George Washington's fellow soldier, Anthony Wayne.

A bold fighter, Wayne distinguished himself during the Revolutionary War by consistently advising a singular strategy.

"Attack."

His zeal earned the exuberant Pennsylvanian the title Mad Anthony Wayne.

Wayne was mad like a fox. During the Revolutionary War,

Washington desired to wrest from the enemy the impenetrable Stony Point, tactically perched above the Hudson River. In a bayonets-only charge that lasted a mere 30 minutes, Wayne led dedicated Patriots up a treacherous cliff and surprised the overconfident British. Following the war for independence, Washington had dispatched the bold Revolutionary War statesman, Brigadier General Wayne, to the frontier to protect settlers from hostile Indians. As he had with his revolutionary tasks, Wayne succeeded in procuring security for those living at the confluence of the Maumee, Saint Mary, and Saint Joseph rivers. Though Mad Anthony's daughter and son grew up with their mother in the Pennsylvania family home, Mallory wondered if her family name could somehow be related to the adventurous man.

Initially, a trading post for Europeans, Fort Wayne sprung up near the peaceful Miami Indian village of Kekionga. Platted in 1823, the city experienced tremendous growth after the completion of the Erie and Wabash canals. Presidential hopefuls Abraham Lincoln and orator Stephen Douglas debated in the city.

A reproduction of Mad Anthony Wayne's 1794 log and chinking fort stood at the junction of the three rivers in the center of the modern city. Mallory knew the history of the city from her school days. Now, as an adult, she knew Fort Wayne derived subsistence from manufacturing, insurance, and health care.

Of particular interest to her were the logistics, defense, and security. Especially the security of one Marc Wayne.

Chapter Thirty-two

Thomas entered Deverell's office.

Chomping hard on spearmint gum, his boss peered questioningly over his glasses. "You found something."

The counter-terrorism specialist nodded.

"Granny, what big teeth you have."

Thomas dropped heavily into a chair across from Deverell. "Initially, the scene looked like a heart attack."

"I remember." Two vertical lines between his eyebrows indicated Deverell's concern. "But?"

"Hatim was diabetic." Thomas paused, thinking. "We found the syringe from the insulin shot he apparently gave himself that evening. Just before he died."

"And?"

"An analysis revealed the contents to be potassium."

"Not insulin?"

"Traces of insulin." Thomas shook his head. "But mostly potassium."

Deverell scratched the back of his neck. "My doctor prescribed a potassium pill each day when I took up jogging."

"Sounds like a personal problem."

"Thank you, Dr. House." Deverell smirked. "Leg cramps were the medical diagnosis."

Thomas nodded. "Not enough potassium, as in your case, has its side effects, including cramps. Additional lack causes blackouts."

"And too much?"

"Too much, as Hatim experienced, causes the heart to stop fairly quickly. It goes through the normal dysrhythmia that a heart would go through when it is dying."

From the bottom drawer of his desk, Deverell selected a bottle and set the vitamins on the desk. The label read potassium. "An overdose of this simulates a heart attack?"

"Hatim injected himself. With tampered insulin."

"And Old MacDonald bought the farm." Deverell tossed the vitamin bottle back into the drawer. "Smart killers."

Chapter Thirty-three

As the plane lined up to touch down on the runway, Mallory took in the bird's-eye view of Fort Wayne. She recognized the General Motors plant, the new strip mall, and the green oblong of a high school football field. Then the plane bumped to the ground and taxied to the gate.

Along the adjacent runway, Mallory heard before she saw the two F-16Cs scream into the sky. Located on the east side of the airport, the 122 Fighter Wing, Indiana Air National Guard base served as home to the Blacksnakes. While a young teen, Marc learned basic rescue and survival skills, as well as how to fly when he participated in the Civil Air Patrol.

"Hey, Sis." She heard Marc call as she followed the flow of passengers into the terminal. On tiptoes, Marc stood behind a collection of overweight relatives gushing welcomes to a young couple in western boots and oversized belt buckles.

"Go left" Marc gave the direction like he used to when they were kids playing flag football. Grinning, Mallory tucked her head and steered around the small crowd. She ran straight into his familiar hug.

"Touchdown," he declared in her ear.

Laughing, she pulled back to get a better look at him. "Hey, Bro."

"Welcome back to Smallville, my big shot sister." He took the handle of her carry-on and, with his arm slung casually around her shoulders, steered her toward the exit.

The revolving door spat them out of the controlled airport air and into the Midwest afternoon. She breathed deeply, welcoming the smell and feel of seasonally mild humidity as they made the short trek to the parking lot. "What's captured your interest lately in that mad scientist lab of yours?"

Marc pressed a button on his key chain, and the trunk of his car popped open. He secured her luggage and opened the passenger door for her. "I've toyed with inventing the barkless dog."

"A toy barkless dog?"

"Toys are mostly barkless. Or you can at least remove the batteries."

"Are Dr. Thurmond's clients getting on your nerves?"

Marc shrugged. "I don't hear 'em really, except today when I spoke on the phone with a new client. A Saint Bernard kept going off like a foghorn."

"That's a unique way for new clients to find your office. Just follow the sound of the barking dog."

"Makes me sound like a hick."

"You are."

He tipped his head. "Ahh. That explains it."

"What about your work with magnetics?"

Leaving the airport parking lot, Marc motored by the day-old bakery and the United Methodist Church. "You mean the Meissner Field Generator?"

"Yeah, that."

He glanced at her. "I thought this was a pleasure trip, negotiated for my patriotic cooperation with the government."

"All the more reason to ask."

He rested his right arm across the back of the seat. "So, is this trip business or fun?"

"Like everything else in my life," she admitted, "some of both."

"Which is why I'm so vital to your life."

"Of course you are, my favorite brother."

"I'm your only brother." He merged the Jetta onto the bypass. "And to remind you how to play, I'm taking you to lunch."

"I should freshen up." She smoothed travel wrinkles from her clothes.

"Hicksville, remember? We suffer from an iron deficiency. That's why all our clothes are wrinkled. You're fine."

Marc parked outside a small storefront attached to a BP gas station. The sign board advertised steak and Chinese food. Mallory sighed. "No one cooks a steak like Bobby."

"And you're overdue for one of your overdones."

Inside, the older waitress greeted Mallory with a hug. "Hi, honey. How are you?"

Mallory returned the hug, happy to see the longtime waitress with the smokey voice. "Well, Nancy."

"Just like she likes her steak," Marc put in.

Guiding them to a booth with green vinyl benches, Nancy nodded. "I remember." She laid two menus on the table.

Marc pushed the menus back to her. "Menus?" His tone was indignant. "We don't need no stinking menus."

The waitress smiled. "Gotcha'. Two usuals comin' right up." She gathered the ignored menus and disappeared. In moments, she returned, balancing a pot of fragrant jasmine tea and a plate of pot stickers and egg rolls.

While Mallory poured tea, Marc dumped a generous portion of sweet red sauce into the center of the plate, topped with a yellow dollop of mustard sauce. Like a painter layering his brush, he expertly dipped an egg roll into the bi-color mixture and handed the miniature masterpiece to his sister.

Mallory bit into the egg roll and closed her eyes appreciatively, savoring the familiar flavors.

"Great, huh?" Marc slathered tangy red sauce on a potsticker for himself.

"A taste of home."

"'Cause no one else would put this menu together," he said around a mouthful. "It wouldn't fly in your fancy DC"

"Nor would this lack of atmosphere."

Marc swallowed. "Are you kidding? The lack of atmosphere *is* the atmosphere."

"Nancy!" someone yelled from the kitchen.

"See?" Marc bit a pot sticker in half. "Where else can you dine and hear the cook holler to the waitress when your meal is ready?" He spoke around the food. "That's atmosphere, baby. Real atmosphere."

Nancy returned and set in front of them plates heavy with steaming steak filets, fried rice, and mixed vegetables.

They were quiet for several minutes, heartily digging into the hot meal. Marc waved his steak knife in Mallory's direction. "Is this good or what?"

She loaded her fork with colorful vegetables. "How's that pretty secretary of yours?"

"Violet?" Marc forked another generous piece of rare steak into his mouth. "Fine, I guess. Why?"

"Just wondering. Is she dating anyone?"

"Dating?"

Mallory looked around and then leaned forward. "Do you hear an echo?"

"What do you mean?"

"Each question I ask about your secretary, you repeat."

"Do I?"

"See."

Marc wiped his mouth with his napkin. "Well, she's… she's… she's Violet. She answers my email, the phone, and makes tea."

"While you…?" She waved her fork for him to fill in the rest.

"While I work. That's what I do, remember. Patents and inventions."

Mallory rested her chin on her palm. "You might want to look up occasionally to see what's right in front of you."

Marc harrumphed.

Nancy replaced their empty plates with a dessert dish piled with crisp fortune cookies and crumbly almond cookies.

Mallory selected a cellophane-wrapped fortune cookie. "So, tell me about your progress on the Meissner Field."

"I've nearly got it, I think." Marc stuffed a whole almond cookie into his mouth and shopped for a fortune cookie.

"That close?"

"Been that close for a while, actually. But the part I don't have, you know, the part I made up for the patent application, that's the part I really don't have."

She stared at him. "That's about the most unscientific explanation I've ever heard from you."

He shrugged. "Occasionally, even this brilliant mind operates like the rest of humanity. Besides, I'm not supposed to talk about it, am I?"

"Except with me."

"I lectured at the university about the Meissner Effect theory—which is common knowledge in the scientific world—but the elements of the invention weren't discussed." He pointed the cellophane-wrapped cookie in her direction. "There was one student who had a natural understanding of the concept. Name's Hebron Heath, and he's already an inventor."

Mallory held up her fortune cookie. "Ready?"

They tore off the wrappers and broke their cookies open. Mallory found her fortune first. "Your life is full of surprises." She frowned. "What does your fortune say?"

Marc studied his small paper. "You will go on a grand adventure."

Chapter Thirty-four

Her belly full from the large lunch, Mallory relaxed in the passenger seat while Marc drove them home. Turning down Maple Street, Mallory leaned forward in anticipation of that first glance of their childhood home.

"The place looks good, Marc." After periods away, her first view always evoked an avalanche of memories and their accompanying emotions. "You've kept it up."

"Naturally. It honors Mom and Dad, but my true motivation," he looked at her conspiratorially, "is to tempt you home now and again."

As soon as he parked, she threw open the car door. She stood in the front room when Marc caught up, tugging her carry-on behind. "It smells like home." She inhaled deeply of her mom's favorite brand of furniture oil. "I can still smell Daddy's pipe."

Taking her by the shoulders, Marc turned her to face the two recliners positioned by the fireplace. "Actually, that's the tobacco on the coffee table next to Dad's easy chair."

She walked to the dish their mom used to fill with candy M & Ms. Vitamin Ms, she called them. Take several each day, hourly if needed. "In the candy dish?"

He closed the front door. "After a while, the place still felt like Mom, but not Dad anymore. Then I found his tobacco pouch."

Mallory blinked. "You are amazing."

He grinned. "I know."

"And modest."

"Humble." He tossed his keys in the air and caught them. "You do whatever women do, and grab a nap. I've got a late appointment, and then I'll be home to challenge you to some basketball hoops."

As he got into the car, Mallory called from the porch. "Tell Violet hello for me."

"Tell her yourself when you come to the office tomorrow morning."

Chapter Thirty-five

The oversized lunch with Mallory had tasted terrific, but now Marc felt sleepy as he worked at his office computer.

Violet appeared. "It's after five." She glanced at his atomic clock. "Nearly five-thirty."

Marc pushed back from his desk and turned his attention to her. Framed in the doorway, her head tipped to one side, she looked fresh, like a spring day, despite the lateness of the afternoon. He wondered if she did have a date that evening. Certainly, someone as pretty and vibrant as Violet had a life outside these dull walls.

"Go on." Why hadn't he wondered about her before? "I'll stay and wait for this last client."

"I can stay until six if you'd like."

"Run along to your real life." He fished, but she didn't take the bait.

"Sure?"

"What could happen?" He made shooing gestures. "I'll see you later." Later? He usually said tomorrow.

She smiled and disappeared down the hall. In a few minutes, he heard the front door close and knew she had gone. The office felt empty. Shaking his head to redirect the curious direction of his thoughts, he left his desk and went to the lab.

Hebron's invention sat on the bench like a question. Marc had played with different theories for the device. Nearly every invention had multiple applications and acted as a natural catalyst for additional developments. And how many ideas had seemingly failed only to become genius in a completely unanticipated venue.

To keep his thoughts off Violet, Marc began a mental list of inventions that had begun with one purpose in mind, only to morph into another use altogether. During World War II, rubber imported from Africa fell into short supply. The United States government needed rubber for airplane and vehicle tires, and to make boots to shoe soldiers. An engineer at General Electric added boric acid to silicon. Instead of rubber, James Wright invented silly putty, a popular child's toy. The putty became the preferred substance for astronauts to anchor floating tools during antigravity space travel.

In 1970, Spencer Silver sought to develop stronger glue for 3M. Instead, he produced the weakest glue yet. Rather like Marc's own recent failed attempt at an adhesive that he washed down the kitchen sink. Perhaps he would find a use for the explosive he had accidentally produced. His kitchen fire reminded him of the fire extinguisher and that reminded him of Violet.

Peering inside Hebron's device, he went back to reviewing his list of redirected inventions. A decade after he created it, Silver's concept became the profitable post-it notes. A favorite office supply of Violet's, she color-coded office projects with bright post-its. This list had not worked as a distraction—he found himself thinking again about Violet.

Marc forced himself to picture the freckled Hebron. Marc's own parents had championed whatever interests he and Mallory favored. In contrast, when the energetic son attempted to connect on common interests, Hebron's father ridiculed and rejected his invention. Marc suspected the father treated his son in much the same way as he regarded his son's creativity.

Spectacular young man. Brilliant invention. There had to be another application for Hebron's device.

His thoughts drifted back to Violet. Maybe she had a dinner date. With someone handsome and athletic. She would smell like spring lavender and wear a dress that flared about her long legs. He had never before thought about Violet going out. Or about taking her out. He shook his head. Not a good idea to date his receptionist. What was he thinking?

Mallory's hints flashed through his memory.

"How is Violet?"

"Say hi to Violet."

What did his sister know that he didn't? He knew Violet to be smart, artistic, and personable. And lovely. Did she like him? Grasping a pair of needle-nose pliers, he lifted Hebron's diamond from the invention's center cradle. Rough, the stone reflected the evening sun that streamed through the window. What other product or industry could benefit from a clarity grading machine?

If he did ask Violet out, Marc would take her some place special. A destination very different from the normalness of their quaint Midwest town. He studied the lenses that focused on the cradle. He might take Violet to the Embassy Theater in downtown Fort Wayne to hear the philharmonic. And to dinner. At an uptown restaurant to impress her. Good food and a bottle of wine. Red.

Wine.

Of course.

Chapter Thirty-six

Back at his desk, Marc completed the email to the professor at the university. After Hebron's great escape from their lunch, he sent a request for the instructor to pass a message to the budding inventor.

Marc hit the send button and directed his focus to the claims to be drafted for a client's patent application. Small numbers at the top of the computer screen read ten minutes after six when Marc heard the front door open.

"Be right with you," he called. Saving his work, he quickly left his office to greet his visitor.

"Marc Wayne," he introduced, extending his hand to the wiry, dark man. "You must be Mr. Spencer."

"I'm pleased to meet you." The man firmly gripped the attorney's hand.

Marc indicated the way to his office. "You can leave your umbrella in the stand by the door."

"I prefer to keep it with me, thank you."

In his office, Marc pointed his guest to a chair. "You've come a long way to see me when we could have done this over the phone."

"You came highly recommended."

Marc took his seat behind the desk. "Tell me about the invention you'd like me to file a patent for."

"Perhaps you could show me what you've been working on?"

Marc hesitated.

The man's tone sounded condescending. "I understand that you have an interest in magnetics. As do I."

"Mr. Spencer, if you are concerned that I might use some of your technical information on my own projects, I assure you—"

"On the contrary," he interrupted. "It would reassure me that you understand my project as you prepare the patent application."

"As a matter of fact," Marc explained, "most patent attorneys and agents are not inventors. An interest in inventing is not a prerequisite to understanding the technology to craft a patent application any more than being a musician is a prerequisite to building fiddles."

"I am merely suggesting an exchange of information." His gaze penetrated. "One inventor to another."

From the front of the building came the sound of the front door opening. "You are expecting another business client." Mr. Spencer rose from his chair.

"Excuse me, please." Marc stood. "I'll be right back."

In the reception area, Marc ran into Violet. "I saw the lights on. Do you need a good secretary while you meet with your client?"

Marc sighed. "Thanks, this squirrel is nutty."

Violet peered around Marc to glance down the hall. "What kind of a nut?"

Marc dropped his voice. "I can't put a finger on it."

"How can I help?" She set down her purse. "Want fresh coffee?"

Marc puffed out his cheeks as he considered her suggestion. "I don't want to encourage him to stay longer than necessary."

"I can interrupt with an important phone call."

Behind her, the door opened again. A handsome man built like a football linebacker came in. "Violet?"

She flushed and turned to the newcomer. "Just a minute, Rob." She turned questioningly back to her boss.

Marc smiled weakly. "Hey, this isn't worth interrupting your plans. I'll handle it."

Rob stepped to Violet's side and slid a possessive arm around her waist. "If you're sure," she offered.

Looking at Rob, Marc nodded. "Yeah, I'm sure."

"Well, you better catch up with your client." Violet glanced again behind Marc. "He disappeared down the hall right after I came in."

"Probably not for the bathroom."

"Probably not."

Marc started for his workroom and then called back to the departing couple. "Thanks for stopping in." He took two more steps before remembering his manners. He turned again, noting that Rob held the door open for Violet. "Nice to meet you… Rob."

As he walked to the back of the building, the deep, rhythmic bark of an aged Labrador sounded from Dr. Thurmond's office next door. But Marc's workshop was empty.

"Mr. Spencer?" Scanning his notes and workbench, he felt confident his visitor had looked the place over. "Mr. Spencer?"

The bolt that usually locked the back door from the inside was unlocked. Marc walked outside. Dr. Thurmond used the grassy area behind the building to walk his quadruped patients. Marc knew to be careful where he stepped.

He scanned the shadows cast by the setting sun and listened for footsteps. He didn't see anything. And the only sound was the Labrador.

Chapter Thirty-seven

Early the next morning, Marc stood outside Mallory's room. Through the closed door, he could hear only silence and knew she slept deeply in her childhood bedroom. No doubt she could use a morning to sleep in and catch up on her rest. Life in the big city resembled a pressure cooker compared to this small town. And her work often demanded she race the clock to outsmart the criminal mind.

Marc left the car for his slumbering sibling and bicycled the country blocks to work. Arriving downtown, he fished a key from his pocket and unlocked the office door. He bent to pick up the newspaper and groaned.

"Are you getting older?" His landlord stood at the doorway of his vet clinic adjacent to Marc's narrow office.

Marc pressed a hand against his lower back and straightened. He glanced sidelong at Dr. Thurmond. "The paper is getting heavier."

Secure in Thurmond's gnarled hands, a beige rabbit wriggled its pink nose. "Weighty news." The vet ran a hand gently down the bunny's back. "In the bottom of the rabbit's cage, it's yellow journalism."

Marc swung his stiff right arm in a wheel. "Mallory challenged me to some one-on-one driveway basketball last night."

At the sound of Mallory's name, Thurmond brightened. "Who won?"

"We didn't keep score," Marc mumbled.

"I thought so." The old man wagged a boney finger. "Be sure she stops in to see me."

"You watch," Marc said. "She'll stop in to see you before she comes here."

A smile lit the man's face, and he winked. "She likes me better."

Marc signaled goodbye with a wave of the newspaper.

Dr. Thurmond became suddenly serious. "Keep a watchful eye on the news."

Chapter Thirty-eight

Seated on a bench outside the local diner, Mr. Spencer adjusted the newspaper he pretended to read.

Wheeling around the corner, Marc Wayne came into view on his bicycle. Squeezing squeaky handlebar brakes, the inventor stopped in front of his office. As he unlocked the front door, an old man appeared from next door. He carried a rabbit in his arms.

Spencer watched the two men exchange animated pleasantries. Then each one retreated into his place of business, closing doors behind them. Instinctively, Spencer remained behind the newspaper for a while longer. Then he carefully folded and left the news on the bench. Grasping his umbrella, he crossed the street and entered the front door of the patent attorney's office.

In moments, Marc met him in the entryway. His expression showed a wariness. "Perhaps," Spencer began, "we can continue from where we left off?"

Marc cleared his throat. "I don't think I can help you."

"On the contrary." Mr. Spencer tilted the umbrella in Marc's direction. "You are exactly the one who can help me."

Marc shifted his weight. "Then you better explain exactly what it is you want me to do for you, Mr. Spencer."

"Of course."

With a sigh, Marc waved his guest ahead of him toward his office.

Mr. Spencer pointed the umbrella, this time toward the hallway. "After you."

Mr. Wayne shrugged and led the way. Mr. Spencer fell into step behind him. Just as the pony-tailed attorney reached his office, Mr. Spencer aimed the umbrella at the back of Marc's right knee. He pressed a hidden trigger, and a small dart shot from the tip and found its target. In seconds, the man in front of him crumbled to the floor.

Perfect. Everything looked to be going according to plan.

Chapter Thirty-nine

Finding the keys on the kitchen table where Marc had left them, Mallory drove the short distance downtown. She parallel parked in front of the historic brick building. As her brother had predicted, she went first to the vet's office.

The bell over the door jangled as she entered. Bent close to a beagle on the examination table, Dr. Thurmond looked up. Spying Mallory, he welcomed her with his throaty chuckle.

"Mallory, my girl. You are a beautiful sight for these old eyes."

She knew the drill. "And just how old are you?"

He came around the table and opened his arms. She walked into his grandfatherly embrace. "Old enough to appreciate when an important woman from the big city takes time to stop by."

She inhaled deeply and smiled against his vet coat. He smelled of Old Spice and iodine. "I'm here for one of your hugs." She pulled back to take in his smiling gaze. "I don't get hugs like this on the East Coast."

"Don't see why not." He patted her shoulder. "You don't smell bad."

The beagle yipped and thumped the tip of his tail on the stainless steel table. "Who's your patient?" Mallory ran a hand over the smooth fur and scratched behind the floppy ears.

"Barney Beagle here cut a foot while chasing rabbits." The vet lifted a front paw and showed her a row of careful stitches mending a crooked tear in the black pad.

"Looks like he'll be back terrorizing Thumpers faster than a DC politician can break his campaign promises."

Dr. Thurmond nodded. "How about you? Are you in town long?"

She looped her arm through his and walked toward the door. "Long enough to collect a few more hugs."

He opened the door for her. "I'm counting on it."

Next door, Mallory breezed into Marc's office. Violet looked up from her desk and smiled. "Mallory." The receptionist came to give her a hug. "How good to see you."

"Violet, you're as lovely as ever. Why you spend your talents here when you could be a million other places is a mystery to me."

Violet blushed and looked expectantly toward the door behind Mallory.

"Don't worry." Mallory pushed the door closed. "I already stopped in to see Thurmond."

Violet's eyebrows came together in a puzzled frown as Mallory turned to go down the hall to Marc's office. "Let's catch up over lunch." She raised her voice and winked at Violet. "Unless you already have a lunch date."

Mallory rounded the corner into Marc's office. Not finding her brother there, she went further down the hall to his workshop where she stood with her hands on her hips. In the room, several projects were in various stages of development. Not as cluttered as usual, on the long workbench lay an array of common tools and parts. But no brother.

"Marc?" She circled the room, trailing her fingers along the back of his tall stool. Returning to the front of the building, she found Violet at her desk, her fingers busy on the computer keyboard. "Where's Marc?"

Violet frowned again. "I thought he was with you."

"When did he leave?"

"He wasn't here when I arrived." Violet looked at his bicycle leaning against the wall next to the umbrella stand. "Just his bike. I figured the two of you went down the street to the grill for breakfast."

"You're probably right. No doubt swapping ideas with the farmers over plates of biscuits and gravy about ways to make their farm equipment function more productively." Mallory opened the front door. "I'll go join him there."

Chapter Forty

The ambulance drove across the airport tarmac toward a private jet.

A half hour earlier, Yao's man had delivered the unconscious inventor in the emergency vehicle. Now the professional mercenary drove while Colonel Yao watched their progress from the passenger seat, a vantage point that allowed him to observe the doctor and patient in the back.

There were four airports in the area.

Situated on 250 acres two miles from Interstate 69, the Colonel had selected Smith Field. Though Fort Wayne's first municipal airport, just prior to the outbreak of World War II, the army purchased a site south of the city for development of an airfield. The new site transformed into the Fort Wayne International Airport, reducing Smith Field to fodder for continued controversy hashed out in the city's newspapers.

From an outsider's view, Yao suspected the media occasionally fanned the fire to create news. Editorials argued that the airport served merely as a taxpayer funded playground for plane owners. He judged the whole affair trivial compared to his responsibilities. Typical Americans. To have so much and fight over the ridiculous when people in his country lacked indoor plumbing and proper medical care.

His research of the four area airports revealed Smith Field to be the smallest with the least amount of traffic. In addition to hosting a weekly meeting for the Civil Air Patrol—moved out of

Blacksnakes headquarters after 9-11—the airport served as an offsite lab space classroom for several colleges that operated a mechanics certification program for high school and college students. Private pilot lessons were available from a sole proprietorship whose owner scheduled lessons over his cell phone while lounging by the pool at a nearby condominium.

The random coming and going of people fit exactly the atmosphere Yao sought. Absorbed in the television, the guy at the airport's small counter easily answered questions, and conveniently for Colonel Yao, didn't ask any.

The ambulance neared the waiting plane where the pilot stood in the fixed-wing's doorway and observed their approach. With graying temples and cropped haircut, Yao suspected the pilot to be retired military.

The driver parked the ambulance next to the plane and moved to the back of the vehicle to help the doctor prepare the patient. Yao approached the pilot who met him on the tarmac.

"Once I have a look-see at the paperwork, we'll get your patient aboard and put this bird in the air."

Yao handed over the required documents. Pushing up his sunglasses to rest on his head, the pilot scanned the forms. Above him, someone appeared in the plane's doorway. Yao looked up and saw his reflection in the dark sunglasses of a woman. She stood unsmiling, her long brunette hair curtained her shoulders.

The pilot slid his sunglasses back over his eyes. "You got a doctor to accompany us and see to the patient?"

From the rear of the ambulance, the doctor appeared and held out his hand to the pilot.

"You the doctor who signed these?" The pilot waved the paperwork.

"And I'll oversee the patient throughout the journey."

"Your nurse?"

Yao winced when the doctor clapped him on the back. "My

assistant."

The pilot grinned. "Well then. Everything is in order." He turned to the woman. "Okay, Babe. Get 'er ready to fly."

The woman turned and disappeared inside. The pilot assisted them in getting the patient secured aboard. The jet turbines began to whine. As they taxied down the runway, from the window, Yao watched the driver get back into the ambulance.

Working with men who reminded him of a cockroach proved a necessary evil, and this one worked with particular efficiency. He had arranged for a medical mercenary who hired himself out to abortion clinics and other unsavory situations. Medical flights required paperwork signed by a physician and demanded a doctor and nurse be aboard. Today, this doctor would keep the patient stable and unconscious. For this service and his discretion, he would be paid substantially.

Watching the ambulance turn out of the airport and onto Ludwig Road, Yao breathed a sigh of relief to be free of Mr. Spencer. For now.

Chapter Forty-one

A purposeful tour of the town, including a return home, produced no brother.

Back at Marc's office, Mallory pretended to be on her cell phone as she waved apologetically at a worried Violet, pointed to the phone, and went straight back to Marc's office.

His laptop was not in the usual place on his desk. Not a good sign. While many men typically brought home their computer to work after hours, Marc never did. He knew when to say enough, lock the office door behind him, and turn his attention elsewhere. He told her that his best ideas for inventions came during the periods when he gave his brain time off. His backpack carried a notepad and myriad pieces and parts he often toyed with at home, but not his computer. Customarily, the laptop remained at the patent attorney's office for correspondence and patent applications.

Stuffing down an urge to panic, she hurried to his workroom. Looking carefully, she noticed an empty spot on his usually cluttered workbench where he stacked his papers scribbled with notes, formulas, and math equations. A thin coat of dust covered the tools and materials scattered to the edges of the workbench. The most used area of the tabletop near Marc's chair had been cleared.

Finding the back door unlocked, she went outside. Two faint lines were visible in the manicured patch of grass leading to the gravel driveway. From her training, she recognized the marks made by heels when someone was dragged. Where the short trail ended, she could see where accelerating dual rear tires had piled dirt.

Cursing, she dialed Thomas. "I think someone took Marc."

Thomas spoke slowly. "Mallory, why would anyone take Marc?"

"He's gone, Thomas. Gone." She traced the path through the grass once more and studied the tracks in the gravel.

"Let's consider options and conclusions."

Despite her struggle for self-control, she felt herself tremble. "People don't just disappear here. There's no place to hide an Easter egg. This town is so small you can't open a car door without hitting someone, let alone—"

"Okay, Mallory." Thomas interrupted the escalating soprano in her voice. "Calm down."

"He's gone. His notes are gone. His laptop is gone. And there's evidence that someone was dragged from his office."

Chapter Forty-two

During the six-hour flight to Southern California's John Wayne Airport, the doctor monitored the patient and kept him hydrated and asleep.

The pilot's unsmiling wife came back to offer prepackaged corned beef sandwiches, round-cheeked red apples, individual bags of Seyfert chips made in Fort Wayne, and pop cans of the Midwest's highly caffeinated drink of choice—Mountain Dew.

After lunch, the pilot spent time in the bathroom before coming back to the cabin. "How's our patient?"

The inquiry Yao dreaded. Before he could answer, the doctor spoke up.

"Resting comfortably, thanks to your flying expertise." The doctor flashed the pilot a toothy smile. "How long have you been doing medical flights?"

"Well now," the pilot looked to the ceiling while he calculated. "First the military, then some time traveling the country, then I hooked up with a doctor here in Fort Wayne who needed a pilot to transport diabetes patients to regular therapy in Nashville. Did that run until he retired, then went into business for myself."

"A while then."

"I'm not exactly in diapers if that's what you mean." He reached for another can of Mountain Dew and popped open the tab. He pointed the can toward Yao. "What about you? What's your story?"

The doctor looked at Yao, and Yao could see amusement in his eyes. "I received my training in university." Yao's practiced English was free of an Asian accent.

"Saw a lot of guys quit college." The pilot took a long swig from his soda. "Some can't sit still that long. For me, that degree meant I could travel faster and farther."

Yao steered the conversation back to safer ground. "How is our flight time?"

"Like I promised, we're a bit ahead of schedule." His eyes went back to the patient. "What's his story?"

Yao nodded towards the pilot's drink. "Could we have a couple of those?"

"Where's my manners?" The pilot retrieved two more cold cans and tossed them to Yao and the doctor.

"Thanks." The doctor opened the can that spit yellow liquid on the front of his shirt. "Stuff looks like horse piss."

The pilot guffawed as the doctor pulled a roll of gauze from his bag. "So, is that good lookin' brunette yours, or can I ask her out?"

The pilot sobered. "Hands off, mate. She's mine all right. Married her as soon as I met her."

"Smart man." The doctor brushed at his shirt. "She'd make a fine nurse."

"A sight prettier than the one you're working with." The pilot eyed Yao.

"Treat her right," the doctor warned, "or I'll offer her a better job."

The pilot grinned and retreated to his cabin. Without the pilot's probing, Yao relaxed. The doctor smiled smugly at Yao, then settled back and closed his eyes for a nap.

Chapter Forty-three

Back at her family home, Mallory wore a path on the carpet. At last, Thomas came on the phone line.

"You're pacing," Thomas stated over the speaker.

"Aren't you?" She snapped back.

"Hold your horses, Deverell just walked in."

Though barely noon, she felt exhausted from keeping her panic at bay.

"We've notified the authorities to be on the lookout for Marc." Deverell sounded in control, but she heard the rapid clicking of his pen. "They're watching airports and freeways."

For the millionth time, Mallory raked her fingers through her disheveled hair. "That's all we're doing? Watching airports and freeways?"

Thomas sounded patronizing. "Mallory, you know the drill. We're doing all we can, and we're doing all we can thoroughly."

"This isn't just anybody that falls under policy. This is my brother."

"We're aware of that, Mallory. Too aware." Deverell's tone reminded them that he hadn't thought involving Marc to be a good idea in the first place.

"This is not about blame." Thomas spoke calmly into the highly charged emotional conversation. "This is about gathering information and finding Marc." He paused. "Now, Mallory, what else can you tell us?"

Mallory took a deep breath. "I've told you everything.

Several times."

"All right." Deverell began his to-do list. "We need you to let his secretary—"

"Violet. Her name is Violet."

"Violet," Deverell repeated. "Let Violet, and anyone else who would be interested, know that Marc has been called away."

"Called away for what? To get his nails done? Pass a kidney stone? Make a speech to Congress? I know, I'll tell them he ducked into a phone booth, changed into his superman cape and flew off to save the world."

"Mallory," Thomas interrupted. "We understand you are upset. And understandably so. But we need you to set your personal feelings aside and put on your professional hat."

"Your big girl panties," Deverell said.

"You are good at what you do," Thomas continued. "Get on the team with us and let's do what we do best. Let's find your brother together."

"Stop pacing and sit down," Deverell ordered.

Mallory dropped onto the couch. "Okay." She pressed the cell phone close to her ear. "I'll let Violet and Thurmond know—"

"Thurmond?" Mallory could hear Deverell's gum snap through the receiver. "What's a Thurmond?"

"The vet next door."

"What's he got to do with any of this?"

Mallory sighed. "He and Marc talk each morning. He'll notice if Marc is gone."

"Great," Deverell said. "Tell the secretary, the vet, the postman, the gas station owner, Curly, Moe, and Larry, the three little pigs, and the muffin man. Whoever."

Chapter Forty-four

Colonel Yao felt relieved when the plane began its descent. Remaining awake for the majority of the trip he found challenging. The smooth flight and the drone of the humming engines tempted him to doze, especially since he'd had little sleep for the past several nights. Making tactical arrangements had proved taxing.

From the window, he watched the John Wayne airport come into view. Unlike Smith Field, this Southern California airport served three million commercial passengers annually through direct flights with easy domestic and international connections. One of the top five busiest general aviation centers in the world, the Santa Ana based terminal served as an important aircraft manufacturing and flight-training center, and played host to several large airlines. Frequent fliers included air cargo carriers transporting 50,000 tons of goods yearly, as well as Life Flight donor organ and critical care patient delivery. That last feature had interested Yao.

Characteristic of a medical flight, the pilot smoothly executed the flare to let the plane settle on the runway and then taxied to a tarmac beside a hangar.

As planned, a second ambulance met the travelers. The smooth-talking doctor handed Yao the IV that fed glucose into the patient's veins and supervised as medics moved the patient.

Once they were settled in the second emergency vehicle and on the road, Yao studied the scenery. Entering Long Beach, the view became a jungle of concrete and industry. Small fast-food stores were squeezed between large and colorless industrial structures. Next to an In and Out Burger stood a silver-plating company. The ambulance turned into the alleyway and stopped in front of an oversized set of metal doors. The driver gave a short blast on his horn, and someone on the inside raised the door high enough to admit the vehicle. In a moment, the ambulance parked inside the gray interior.

Stepping out the passenger door, Yao observed the surroundings. A cement floor with metal walls. Above two waist-high tanks hung cranes built to lift heavy cargo and lower the pieces into the plating tanks. But today the rusty cranes loomed still over empty tanks.

"This was successful in its day." The ambulance driver dug a cigarette pack from his shirt pocket. "But shortly after the environmental groups began watch-dogging the industry, that larger tank sprung a leak. Seeped into the ocean before they found it."

"Unfortunate." Yao refused the cigarette the man offered.

"Not for me." Like a thirsty man needing a drink of water, he took a long pull on the lit cigarette. He waved the pack in the direction of the ambulance before dropping the box back in his pocket. "Can't smoke in that. Rules about asthmatics, you know."

Yao frowned as the metal door slid closed once more.

"Don't worry." The man blew a lungful of smoke. "We're a couple minutes ahead of schedule." He kicked the empty tank. "Naturally, the place got shut down, and the city is trying to figure out what to do with it. The current plan is to make this a shelter for the homeless to bed down."

"Until then, you put it to use."

The man spread his hands in a mock bow. "What can I say? I'm a businessman."

"A real entrepreneur."

Outside, another short horn blast sounded, and Yao's portly

companion crushed out his cigarette under his heel as he signaled for the door to be raised. On their tracks, the rollers echoed loudly, lifting along the ceiling to reveal a hearse waiting outdoors. Yao glanced at his watch. Right on time.

The elongated car parked, and a solemn man emerged from the driver's side. He approached as the metal door slid back down, trapping inside the smell of exhaust and cigarette smoke.

Efficiently, the doctor and the newcomer positioned the patient inside a satin-lined coffin. The doctor checked the patient's vital signs, nodded to Yao, and the coffin was loaded into the shiny hearse, as gray as the building they were in.

The ambulance driver slapped the doctor on the back. "I'll get you back to the airport before I return this buggy."

The door opened again, and the hearse pulled out. Once more in the passenger seat, Yao watched the ambulance driver take another cigarette from his pack and offer one to the doctor. Another reason Yao tolerated the vile Mr. Spencer was that he arranged the payments to the people who provided services that facilitated the Colonel's plans. Usually that meant an amount up front, padded with a don't ask, don't tell stipulation. The final payment appeared in their bank account when the job was complete. Hirelings weren't tempted to bargain with or threaten Yao over something as trivial as money. Careful that the money trail would not lead back to him, Yao never dealt with the sordid financial arrangements. Yao focused on the plan.

The hearse navigated down the alley, turned right on the street, and drove toward the Pacific Ocean.

Soon they arrived at the Long Beach pier. Though not yet out of danger, Yao began to breathe easier. Chinese shipping conglomerates owned sections of the harbor, and the hearse steered to one of these. Looming ahead, a hulking cargo ship lay pulled tight against the dock. On the gangplank, several men loaded cargo. Like a giant praying mantis, a crane hoisted a shipping container aboard and stacked the container like a child stacks blocks.

A short, blocky man with a gap between his front teeth, the Captain greeted Yao. "Colonel, welcome aboard." He studied the hearse. "I'll have my men load your belongings, and we'll ship out." The Captain signaled to a uniformed sailor. "This man will take you to your quarters."

Yao waved away the sailor. "After my things are aboard."

"As you wish." The Captain watched as four men carried the coffin up the gangplank.

As the hearse departed, Yao turned and followed the coffin to his quarters. Conditions, the captain assured as they proceeded, would be sparse but adequate.

As soon as the casket was secure in a room near his own, Yao dismissed the Captain. "And send the ship's doctor here."

Chapter Forty-five

After searching for additional clues behind Marc's office, Mallory returned home to think in the quiet. As she paced in the living room, the smell of her dad's tobacco multiplied her feelings of guilt. The last thing she ever wanted to do was disappoint her loving parents. This time she hadn't wrecked the family car. She had lost her brother. And not just lost him, he had been kidnapped by ruthless enemies. She didn't want to imagine his fate if she didn't find him.

What had she gotten Marc into? What began as a simple information plant to track and trap a spy had exploded, and she wasn't sure where to find the pieces.

The enemy had proven to be far more dangerous than she and Thomas had predicted while they sat in their comfortable conference room on the East Coast. Underestimating the opponent had resulted in the death of Hatim Saad and Marc's abduction. As she mentally raced through possible scenarios, she feared he would be tortured and killed, and she would never find him.

Her phone chirped, and Mallory jumped even though she had been expecting the call.

"Anything new in your neighborhood, Mallory?" Thomas's familiar voice was a comfort.

"Nothing, Thomas. What have you come up with?"

He cleared his throat. A stalling device, she discerned. "I've been in touch with local law offices in Indiana, and they don't have anything, either. They'll let us know if something suspicious shows up."

Mallory kicked the couch. "I can't believe these creeps pulled this off without any trace. Look at the reports again, Thomas. You must have missed something."

"I'm telling you, Mallory—"

"And I'm telling you to look again."

"All right." She could hear Thomas mumbling as he revisited the reports.

"Something," Mallory pleaded. "Anything to show me where to look next."

Thomas chuckled.

"I can't believe you think this is funny, Thomas. How can you be so callous—"

"Whoa, Mallory. Calm down, I'm not laughing at the situation. Just a note in the police log."

From the front window, she could see the basketball hoop in the driveway. The hoop where she and Marc had played one-on-one just last night. Their games were spirited and underhanded, and the score was usually disputed which led to a play-off. That was the thing about Indiana. A house may or may not have appliances, but every address had a basketball hoop. Hoosiers had priorities, after all. "What does it say?"

"An ambulance waited at the mechanic's for routine maintenance. The mechanic reported the vehicle missing from their parking lot, but when the police stopped by to take a report, the ambulance was right where it was supposed to be." He laughed again. "In the big city, mechanics smoke their lunch, not their breakfast."

Mallory twisted a strand of hair around her finger. "An ambulance," she whispered.

"What? What did you say, Mallory?"

"That's it. That's how they got him out of town." She spun back to face the room. "They took him in an ambulance."

Thomas whistled. "No one would check an ambulance."

Mallory switched the phone to her other ear and reached for a pen and paper. "Where would an ambulance take Marc?"

"A hospital? Paramedic headquarters? Shoot, Mallory, an ambulance can go wherever it wants."

In handwriting shaky with anticipation, Mallory listed the places he said and added several ideas of her own. "Wherever it wants," she echoed. "They'll take him out of the country."

"The quickest way to do that is by air."

"Of course! A medical flight."

"They could move a body without many questions," Thomas conceded. "I'll follow up on medical flights out of all the nearby airports."

"Still, no flights from our local airports are international. There has to be a connection."

"Fort Wayne is an international airport."

She snorted. "A misnomer. Or positive thinking by the city planners that gave the place the name. It's still too small to handle anything that big. Medium sized and commuter connections only." She snapped her fingers. "Indianapolis is two hours away. Detroit or Chicago airports are three to four hours away."

"If I was grabbing a guy, I'd want to get him as far away from the area where people would be looking for him as quickly as possible. My vote, Mallory, is that they got Marc on a plane locally. Besides, the vehicle was back at the mechanic's by the time the police came by. Maybe an hour. Two at most."

She scratched several airports off the list. "That rules out Indianapolis or Detroit or Chicago. Travel would take all day to get there and back."

"That fits with my theory for a local connection." Thomas paused, thinking. "These guys are flying under the radar, attracting as little attention as possible."

"Getting a guy out of the country by commercial air would be tricky. What about a boat?"

"Boat would take longer," Thomas considered. "From the East Coast or from the West Coast?"

"No telling." Mallory dropped onto the couch. "The Great Lakes are only two hours away, and that would get them to Canada."

"We'll have the Coast Guard inspect outgoing vessels bound for foreign ports."

"Right away, Thomas. Don't waste a minute."

"Come on back to the office, Mallory. We'll follow the trail better from here."

She shook her head. "Not until I find a trail here. I know their jumpin' off place began in Dixon."

Chapter Forty-six

Hebron checked for addresses along the Main Street in the small town of Dixon. At last, he found the one that matched his computer search for intellectual property attorney Marc Wayne. The elongated brick building with character, completely unlike conventional law offices, appeared bland and businesslike. Hebron liked it.

Inside, a pretty lady at the reception desk greeted him. "Can I help you?"

If he wasn't imagining things, Elvis Presley played from an eight track. "I'd like to see Mr. Wayne."

She got up and came to him. "He is out of the office right now. Can I take a message?"

Hebron adjusted the backpack slung over his shoulder. "My professor said Mr. Wayne wanted to talk about my invention."

She introduced herself. "Is Mr. Wayne preparing a patent for you?"

"Don't think so. He has my device, a round object about this big." He held out his hands to indicate the size. "Said he found another use for the design besides categorizing diamonds."

She brightened. "He had that in his workshop. Come on back, and you can identify it."

She led the way to an open room at the rear of the building. The size of his dorm at college, the room's walls were lined with low shelves topped with counters and crowded with grouped materials. In the center of the room, a stool sat in front of a worktable. In addition to the overhead lights, a direct light on a flexible stand was clipped to the edge of the table. Dusty yellow legal pads with sketches and formulas were stacked beside books and computer printouts with information on magnetics, magnetic fields, and propulsion systems.

"Cool." Hebron circled the room. "Very cool."

Resting her hand on the empty place on the table, Violet frowned. "Marc worked with your project. But I don't see it now."

Hebron took this as an invitation to look through the creative space.

"It was right here," Violet mumbled, and Hebron wondered if she was talking to him or to herself. He decided to believe she spoke to herself, so he didn't have to formulate a hypothesis about a question he didn't have the answer to. Clearly, she seemed puzzled, though he didn't understand why.

"Why would this area be cleared?" Violet continued in the low tone he anticipated to be reserved for herself. "Marc collects so much material, I need to rent an extra room from Thurmond for storage."

"What's a Thurmond?"

Now Violet circled the room, looking over and under shelves, cabinets, and counters. "Who. Who is Thurmond?" Back to where she began, she stopped and bent to look under the worktable. "Dr. Thurmond is the landlord."

"Does he have a dog?" Hebron cocked his head toward the common wall that separated Marc's office from the other side of the building. From that side came the mournful bay of a hunting dog.

"Depends on the day." She rested her hand on her hips. "Yesterday he had a goat next door."

"Kidding?"

"Not even."

A stack of magnets caught his attention, and Hebron flipped

through the notes on the legal pad. He recognized symbols relating to the Meissner Effect. He scanned theories about projecting a Meissner Field.

"Brilliant."

"What's that?" Violet peered at the pages.

"Projecting the Meissner Field will levitate. Objects will float. Like a submarine in water."

"I didn't think that invention was an underwater vehicle."

Hebron shook his head. "Theoretically, a Meissner device is a superconductor." He squinted. "Okay, not exactly a superconductor in the traditional way the title is applied. The machine would reject magnetic fields, sort of an anti-magnetic field." He reached for two magnets and held them, so they repelled. "The design would repel magnetic fields like a submarine displaces water in its ballast to give the machine buoyancy in water."

"The way a jet moves through air."

Hebron and Violet turned to see a professional-looking woman in the doorway. The college student grinned. Someone who spoke his language. "Exactly. Magnetic currents flow across the earth's surface, similar to the currents in the ocean. Giving the machine buoyancy on earth, the device will generate an exclusionary field, like a bubble, that excludes the planet's natural magnetic currents."

Violet stepped between the two and made introductions.

Hebron stuck out his hand, but Mallory refused his handshake. Instead, she folded her arms. "You have an unusual understanding of Marc's theory."

Feeling awkward, Hebron stuffed his hands into his jeans pockets. "He gave a lecture at the college, and we talked more about the idea over lunch." He motioned to the pads of notes. "Once the foundation of the theory is grasped, the rest unfolds."

"Ah." Mallory unfolded her arms. "Marc told me about you."

Violet picked up yesterday's mug, still half full of cold Earl Grey. "Did he tell you where Hebron's invention is?"

Chapter Forty-seven

Marc's head pounded. He'd had a few migraines in his day, and this felt like one on steroids. He tried to move, but his body refused to respond.

At first, he thought he felt dizzy. But the irregular yet rhythmic sway continued. From the exterior sound of a throaty whistle, he surmised he floated aboard a ship. That didn't compute. How many ships were in Indiana? Certainly, plenty of ski and pontoon boats dotted the one hundred or so lakes in his Midwest state, but none of them had a whistle so deep that the tone resonated in his chest.

Breathing deeply, he inhaled the briny smell of salty ocean water. Far from Indiana, the ocean lay either far to the east or farther still to the west. Or south. Either option caused a wave of panic to flood his veins.

His eyelids felt too heavy to lift, which added another baffling fact. He squeezed his eyes tight and tried to remember. Why would he be in a boat on the ocean? He recalled Mallory had come for a visit. He pictured himself bicycling to work as usual. He had chatted with Thurmond. Then he went into his office. Violet wasn't in yet. A typical day so far.

Another long and deep whistle sounded, followed by the indignant shrill of seagulls. He heard the hum of the vessel's engine purr to life beneath him. A fresh wave of alarm made him nauseas. He fought the pounding in his head as he again struggled to recollect what brought him to this situation. He had been in his office. At the computer. He remembered that the bell jangled over the front door.

Slogging through his sluggish memory felt like trying to run a marathon in a swimming pool. With great effort, he determined to take the next step. The front bell had rung. That meant someone had come in. Thurmond? No. Violet? No. Mallory? No. He took a deep breath and tried to relax. To slow the pounding of his heart fueled by fear. To invite his memory to release its panicked stranglehold on the information he sought.

Someone had come into the office the night before. The same person who came in that morning. Someone who made him uneasy.

"I don't think I can help you."

"On the contrary, you are exactly the one who can help me."

Mentally, he repeated the conversation several times but still couldn't picture who had said that last line. Turning his head, he felt an arrow of pain zing through his temple. The sensation reminded him of being stung by a bee. Once as a kid swimming in a pool. And again in the back of his knee. He had been walking and someone walked behind him.

"On the contrary, you are exactly the one who can help me."

An eerie image wavered in his memory.

Mr. Spencer.

But why would Mr. Spencer want him on a ship?

Chapter Forty-eight

"We are near international waters, Colonel Yao." The Captain flashed a grin that showed the gap between his front teeth.

Yao stood on the bridge near the Captain's elbow. With every passing mile between himself and the California shoreline, he breathed a little easier. Once he knew they were safe from inspection, he planned to retreat to his cabin and celebrate with several shots of tequila. He would need at least that much for his tense muscles to relax. He could use several hours of solid sleep, too.

Confident everything had proceeded according to schedule, Yao left the bridge. Out of sight of the crew, he wearily made his way to his quarters. Inside, he undid the top button of his shirt and poured that long anticipated shot. A taste he'd acquired in college, he only allowed himself to enjoy tequila on rare occasions. In a single fluid motion, he downed the bitter liquid and poured himself a second as a frantic knock echoed at the door.

"We're being boarded." The Colonel recognized the breathless crewmember from the bridge.

"Boarded?" Yao hated inane questions and was well aware he'd just asked one. "I understood we were past the limit."

"Almost, sir. We were nearly at the twelve-mile limit. But a Coast Guard boat from the United States has contacted us that they will board for an inspection in moments."

As if to prove the man's words, the Colonel heard the ship's engines slow.

"Captain thought you'd want to know." The seaman jogged back down the passageway.

Yao hurried into the adjacent cabin where Marc Wayne, deep in a medically induced sleep, rested in a bunk.

Chapter Forty-nine

Having searched Marc's office for anything she had missed, Mallory felt disappointed she hadn't found anything. Brooding, she collected her brother's bike and loaded the simple transportation into the trunk of Marc's Jetta. As she did with the two-wheeler, Mallory wanted to take Marc back home where he belonged. To be in the secure haven of their family homestead, play some driveway basketball, and go out to eat at the restaurant where Bobby would cook her steak to perfection and holler for Nancy to take the tasty feast to the diners. She would talk about Violet. Then he could one day marry and make Mallory an aunt.

Anxiety and regret churned her stomach so that she wondered if she would ever be able to eat again. Mallory had concocted a plausible story for Violet. Always smelling of spring, the receptionist would continue to run the office, and Mallory felt confident Violet would do her usual efficient job. Two years behind Marc in school, Violet was smitten, and Marc remained the only person clueless about her feelings.

Typical, really, for the inventive personality. Living with Marc all her life, Mallory had met his friends. Even in college, Marc and his circle of engineers, computer geeks, and mathematicians were exuberant about their scientific discoveries and content to relate to women in a purely academic setting. Like Jimmy at work, behind their back, these guys were called late bloomers on the topic of noticing females as potential romantic interests.

Beautiful and smart, Violet knew better than to share her feelings with the object of her affection. Marc would be embarrassed and avoid her like the repelling end of one of his magnets. Patient, she unobtrusively orbited him and invested her talents making a reputation in the community as the patent attorney's sunny assistant who got things done. One day, Marc would decide he would like to share his life with someone special. But the timing would be later than the average single guy. Far from average, Marc existed on a different plane than most. To love such an eccentric would require a unique woman.

Pulling into the driveway of the home where she and Marc had grown up, Mallory's strained spirits plummeted. The house looked dark. No one was home. Mom and Dad were gone. And thanks to her strategy as the lead on her first project, her irresponsible planning had gotten Marc kidnapped. She had robustly underestimated the power and determination of the thieves and spies she sought. Chastising herself for mistaking international black-market dealers for computer geeks who had merely hacked into the United States Patent and Trademark Office, Mallory realized in her idealism, she had stereotyped the crime. Historically, such a misstep was a career-buster at best and disastrous for all concerned at worst. Driven by pride, such amateur behavior got people killed.

She wheeled the bike inside to the usual spot near the front door. This action would be the single normal task in the day, putting Marc's bicycle in the place where the two-wheeler normally parked. Perhaps, if she put enough pieces into normal slots, their lives that were suddenly spinning wildly out of control would find the well-worn path back, too.

Drawing the drapes, the night closed in, and she wrapped the dark around her. Everything felt gloomy, heavy, and hopeless. Sitting on the couch, she wondered what to do now? After messing up the situation beyond recognition, she felt tempted to surrender to the overwhelming depression that beckoned. To be completely female and have a good cry where no one would see.

Instead, she cursed. Loud, bitter words as she paced through the house. Going from room to room, Mallory recalled family traditions and berated herself for being incompetent as an FBI agent, as a daughter, and as a sister. She cringed, horrified by the power of the faceless foes that had invaded her world and stolen the person who meant the most to her. And she felt terrified. Fearful of what could happen to Marc, and frightened to be so utterly out of control.

Breathless and spent, she sagged against the hallway wall and slid to the floor. Resting her head back against the hard surface, she faced the extensive collection of family photos her mom had yearly framed and hung. Her mother had dubbed the expanding collection the Wall of Fame.

The smiling eyes of her parents looked out at her. "I'm sorry, Mom and Dad. Really sorry."

Chapter Fifty

Commander Luc Gennett ordered the United States Coast Guard Cutter *Resolute* alongside the cargo ship. The medium endurance ship had been nicknamed by drug smugglers, El Tiburón Blanco; Spanish for The White Shark.

A sailor delivered the commander's meal from the galley as Gennett reviewed his orders on the bridge. Inspect foreign ships in US waters, particularly looking for an American passenger named Marc Wayne. Apparently, Gennett's superiors believed Mr. Wayne could be aboard against his will. While search and rescue remained common for the Coast Guard, this type of hunt fell outside of the ordinary.

Career military, Commander Gennett had enlisted to get as far away as he could from the Iowa pig farm where he grew up. He didn't want his father to think for one nanosecond that his second-born son had any intention of joining the family livestock business. That decision had been made the day a piglet fell into the muck under the pig barn, and 13-year-old Luc had to dive into the smelly pool of pig poop, slop, and water to retrieve the slippery, squealing baby porker.

Much to his older brother's delight, Luc emerged, gripping the pig by a back leg and holding his own stomach as he retched uncontrollably for the next several hours. His clothes had to be burned and despite multiple hot showers and thorough scrubbings with enough lye soap to remove the top layer of skin, it was weeks before Gennett was free of the stench. It was months before he no longer gagged every time his brother brought up the topic, usually any time the girls paid more attention to the younger and handsome Luc than to his tormenting older sibling.

From that day forward, Luc had sworn off pork and never reconsidered, even when the ship's cook served fat sausage links and juicy bacon for breakfast.

"Eat while it's hot." The sailor removed the cover that kept today's meal warm. Next to a helping of scalloped potatoes with bits of bacon were a serving of green beans with pork pieces and two thick slices of brown sugar ham.

Solemnly, Gennett replaced the cover over the offending plate. "Take it away. I'm not hungry."

"Sir?" The younger man's expression looked pained.

"Did you already eat?"

"Yes, sir." Wistfully, the sailor eyed the tray.

Swallowing against his childhood memories from the pig farm, Gennett scanned his orders once more. "You would do me a service if you could polish that off as well. Wouldn't want to offend the cook."

"Sir, no, sir." Eagerly, the sailor reached for the fork.

Gennett stopped him with a look. "Away from here. Enjoy your meal somewhere else."

The sailor complied. Though he had quickly left with the tray, the aroma of pork lingered. Gennett pinched closed his nostrils and exhaled long. Catching the curious sidelong glance of the helmsman, Gennett mumbled something about allergies and refocused on the task at hand.

As the *Resolute* neared the cargo tanker, Coast Guardsmen on deck prepared to secure the two boats together. From his post on the bridge, Gennett watched the procedures and recalled his earlier standards. When he decided to enlist as a means to get away from the family farm, not just any branch of the military service would suffice. The pig farmer's son chose the branch that boasted the most action.

"The United States Coast Guard is one of seven uniformed services," the recruiter had told the teenaged Gennett at a career fair. "Uniquely, the Coast Guard is also a maritime law enforcement agency with jurisdiction in domestic and international waters."

"What's that mean?" Gennett wanted to be certain about what he agreed to before he signed. Previous experience had made him cautious before he dove in.

"It means we are a federal regulatory agency, part of the Department of Homeland Security." The recruiter unfolded a colorful brochure. "Though we are the smallest armed service, our mission is to protect the public, the environment, the economic, and security interests of the nation."

"What's that look like?"

The recruiter with cropped salt and pepper hair had pointed to a picture. "It looks like we don't take slackers. While most military services are either at war or training for war, the Coast Guard is deployed every day."

While Luc had meticulously filled out paperwork, the recruiter made small talk. "Have any diving experience?"

"Some."

"Most of our work is in the sea." He glanced at Luc's address. "Being from Iowa, you probably have freshwater experience."

Luc shook his head. "Definitely not fresh water."

Chapter Fifty-one

Marc felt like he was swimming up through a sea of molasses as he fought for consciousness. Like a bad dream, the harder he worked the more the surface eluded him. The light of awareness danced close for a moment and then reeled far away. Reaching, pulling, kicking, he worked to break through. Finally, he grasped the evasive, shimmering objective.

At last, he opened his eyes. His head thundered like a massive hangover. He hadn't drank enough to be hung over since college. As a student, once had been enough to swear off too much alcohol ever again. Why people considered a night of being out of control followed by a bout of illness worse than food poisoning to be fun did not compute with him.

Though his limbs were still drugged, too heavy to move, he could will a response from his neck. Gingerly, he turned his head to get his bearings. Marc's heartbeat pounded in his ears as he looked at the simple surroundings comprising a small, colorless room with a round nautical window. The droning of large engines reminded him of his earlier impression of being aboard a ship.

The door opened, and he quickly closed his eyes. He didn't want to alert anyone that he was awake but helpless until he had a better sense of what might be going on and who might be involved. He heard the footsteps of two men enter the room.

"Give him another dose," someone commanded.

"He'll be asleep on that last dose for some time yet, I assure you," came a second voice.

"Give it anyway," said the first. "I can't afford for him to be awake when our guests arrive."

Chapter Fifty-two

Elbows on the kitchen table, Mallory went over her written list of facts. Out of habit, she had brewed a cup of coffee that sat, forgotten and cold, in front of her. The morning news droned from the television. She told herself she had turned on the TV to stay updated, but in truth, the sounds of voices other than her own helped her feel less alone.

Unable to add to, or cross off, anything on her list of possibilities, Mallory poured a fresh cup and walked outside. The crisp autumn air connected sharp and uncomfortable without a jacket, but Mallory needed to feel something rather than the physical and mental numbness she had slipped into last night.

In the backyard, she spotted the fire ring long used for bonfires and roasting marshmallows. The well-used circle served as a gathering place for family evenings, youth group activities, and scouting events. Her mother's garden where her parents spent summers harvesting tomatoes, green beans, and cilantro rested under a blanket of leaves. Beyond that stood the now empty pole barn where Mallory and Marc had raised various 4-H projects including Nubian goats, Jersey Giant chickens, a llama named Dolly, and a soft-eyed cow that grew into the state champ for its enormous size thanks to Marc's scientifically designed diet. One summer's goose eggs, hatched in Marc's homemade incubator, produced a flock of geese and one goose that followed Marc like a puppy. Calling weep, weep as she shadowed Marc, the goose earned the name Fido.

In the pond, Marc had floated all manner of boat designs, raised an annoying pair of muskrats her parents referred to as Suzie and Sam, and became familiar with the microscopic species that made up the unseen aquatic community.

Mallory stuffed her cold hands into her jeans pockets. Her parents had provided a secure and nurturing environment for their two children to grow and develop. Life had been fairly smooth for Marc and Mallory. Until now. Though clearly an excuse, Mallory credited underestimating the opponent to lack of personal exposure to truly difficult situations. She needed an answer, even a poor one, to the persistent why that must be silenced, so she could professionally consider the available information.

Or had her parents sheltered her from their adult worries? The result of his mother's bout with measles when he was in utero, her father had been born without legs below his knees. Born to an Amish couple, her dad was never expected to walk. But before age two, like most toddlers, he pulled himself up on his half legs and taught himself to walk. The rest of his life had been a series of prosthesis, those that fit and those that did not.

With fresh appreciation, Mallory surveyed the fire ring, garden, barn, and pond. All were designed and built by a man without feet. Back inside, she stood again in front of the Wall of Fame. A portrait showed the four of them, her father with his cane. Her parents met at the Fort Wayne Embassy Theater. Her mother recalled their father as looking quite dapper when she first saw him with his gold-topped cane in the ornate lobby of the city's grand landmark. Their wedding photo occupied the center place on the Wall of Fame.

The happy couple welcomed the birth of Mallory. But two years later, her mother fought for her life when their second child died at birth. His tiny heart beat too weak to sustain life outside the womb where his mother's body had tenderly supplied the circulation he needed. The diagnosis revealed that Mallory's mom had lupus. Grieving the loss of their longed-for infant son, they also grieved that the young woman would carry no more babies.

The next several years were dark and filled with the uncertainty of another day of life together before the lupus could be managed. Then Marc joined their family, adopted and arriving with the unlimited potential that comes with all newborns. For the first time, Mallory considered what reality had been like for her parents to succeed in life perpetually challenged by her father's limiting physical handicap and her mother's incurable disease.

But they had thrived. Those two intrepid spirits had faced their trials. Without a path to follow, her parents had set the goal to build a wholesome family and future, and navigated a trail. The final portrait Mallory had taken of her parents standing together next to Dad's heirloom Eiffel tower rose. With the help of Marc's fertilizer recipe, the fragrant pink blossom topped a six-foot-tall stem.

No matter what the setback, or the hindrance, Mr. and Mrs. Wayne refused to be detained. Handicapped, they were not crippled. Standing before the photographic tribute to the character of her parents, Mallory determined she would never give up. She would find her brother.

Her phone rang. The excitement in Thomas's voice quickened her pulse. "Mallory, I located a medical flight that left the area right after Marc disappeared."

Chapter Fifty-three

In a handful of years, Gennett quickly rose through the ranks to captain his own vessel. As an enlisted member, that journey included a stint at Officer Candidate School.

Alexander Hamilton founded the Revenue Cutter Service on August 4, 1790, making the Coast Guard the nation's oldest continuous seagoing service. The Guard's founding mission outlined collecting taxes from a new nation of patriot smugglers. When at sea, the officers were instructed to crack down on piracy. During those duties, they might as well rescue anyone in distress.

After the September 11, 2001, terrorist attacks against the United States, the Coast Guard formed The Deployable Operations Group. The DOG brought numerous existing deployable law enforcement, tactical, and response units under a single command headed by a rear admiral. The unit contained several hundred highly trained Coast Guardsmen whose missions include maritime law enforcement, anti-terrorism, and port security.

As captain of his own vessel, Gennett served as one of nearly 50,000 active duty members who were supported by another 10,000 reservists, nearly the same number of full-time civilian employees, and 30,000 active auxiliary members. The Coast Guard's decentralized organization and readiness for missions made the service highly effective, extremely agile, and adaptable in a wide range of emergencies.

Of French descent, Gennett had a slight build and sandy colored hair. Deep lines were etched around his eyes from years of squinting into the sun. Now he peered through binoculars at the Chinese vessel. The large ship had any number of shadowy places where a man could hide. Or be hidden.

Much as a traffic cop checks the record of a speeding driver, the *Resolute* radioed for information about the tanker. Gennett readied his boarding team.

Chapter Fifty-four

Late afternoon the day after Marc's disappearance, Mallory mashed the accelerator to the floor. Tires squealed as they slipped, then grabbed, and her car shot forward. The pilot she wanted to talk to, the guy who did medical transports, positioned his plane for takeoff. If that plane got airborne, who knew when she would get another chance to question him.

Smashing through the chain-link fence between the parking lot and the flight field, she skidded around a Cessna as it landed, fishtailed, corrected, and pressed forward. On the far side of the landing strip, her car flattened a runway light and bounced onto the grassy patch. Her tires throwing dirt and grass, she bore down on the second runway.

Moments ago, above the volume of the television, the lanky grandpa at the airport had informed Mallory, "The medic transport plane has just cleared for takeoff."

Glancing out the picture window, she had spotted a fixed-wing rolling into position on the far runway. Now she steered for the middle of the takeoff path. She could hear the plane's engines at full throttle. The aircraft began its race down the asphalt, picking up momentum that would aid in the jet's release from gravity's pull. Mallory turned directly into the on-coming airplane's path and jerked the wheel. Wheels squealing, the car slid sideways and slammed to a stop.

The engines whined as the medical transport reversed engines and turned to avoid a collision. Askew on the pavement, the plane braked to a stop. Mallory released the breath she had been holding and sprinted to the plane. The hatch flew open.

"Can I help you?" A slender man with a military haircut, the pilot leaned coolly in the doorway, a can of Mountain Dew in his hand. "Or are you some kind of crazy?"

Mallory flashed her identification. "I want to see your flight log."

"Of course, you do." The man's agitation reflected clearly behind his sarcasm.

From the cockpit, a woman appeared and handed him the book. She took his place leaning in the doorway, silently watching behind dark sunglasses, while he descended the aluminum steps.

Mallory read through the entries. She focused on their most recent trip. Five souls on board. Travel speed in knots. Weather conditions. Coordinates. "Tell me about your last transport."

"What do you want to know? The paperwork looked neat and tidy. We had the required doctor to patient ratio."

"Who was your patient?"

"Not my business. I'm the pilot." He put a hand on the fuselage. "My job is the plane."

"Did he look like this?" She showed him a photo of Marc.

He shrugged. "I had no interaction with the patient. I did not observe him. Pilots don't do patient care." He closed and tucked the logbook under his arm. "Vital signs, orders for patient care, patient responses—the doctor and nurse do their own charts."

Mallory choked back desperation. She needed some indication of where to search for Marc. She wasn't good at interrogation, but as a research analyst, she had been trained to scrutinize and follow clues. "The patient arrived by ambulance?"

He chugged the last of his drink. "That's usually how it goes with medical transport."

"What time?"

He tapped the logbook. "Early morning. We were in the air

before most folks were at work."

Mallory glanced up. The silent woman stared back at her. Were these people just doing their job, or were they directly connected to Marc's disappearance? If they were involved, it didn't make sense for them to return so quickly to Smith Field. Knowing someone would be looking up his skirt, the pilot would find it advantageous to remain unavailable.

"Describe who was with the patient."

"Not anyone I've flown for before. Doctor was a cocky guy. His nurse was ugly." He laughed at his own joke and then held up his palms. "Not that I'm racist."

"Racist?"

"Not me. I've worked with all kinds in the military and out. Don't care what color they are. I do care how they do their job."

"Did the nurse do her job?"

"He. Did *he* do his job." He motioned to the woman who tossed down a fresh can of Mountain Dew. "Saw a lot of corpsmen in the service but not many male nurses in the real world. The ones that are tend to be a younger group—not concerned with stereotypes. With folks thinking they are wussies."

"The nurse was an older guy. Anything else about him?

"Quiet. But when he did speak, I expected an accent. But spoke as good as you and me."

"What accent did you expect?"

He pointed the can away from Mallory and popped the top. Like a rooster tail, yellow spray splashed on the black asphalt. "Chinese, Japanese, something Asian."

Mallory felt her heart leap into her throat. Asia lay on the other side of the globe. Asia also lined up with the stolen technology that led to China's new jet engine.

"And you took them to John Wayne airport?"

"They were offloaded in time for the Mrs. and me to have a late lunch at the beach."

Mallory raked a hand through her hair. "Yesterday."

He took a swig from the drink can.

She studied him, stuffing her emotions in an attempt to think clear enough to ask professional questions. There had to be something to gain from this pilot before he flew to his next destination. "Anything you can remember about the patient? Anything at all?"

The pilot shook his head.

Mallory turned to leave, but a voice from the plane stopped her.

From behind her sunglasses, the woman answered the question. "He had a ponytail."

Chapter Fifty-five

Fighting dread, Yao watched the Coast Guard ship approach.
Her flag snapped spiritedly in the Pacific wind. Consisting of 16
perpendicular stripes of alternating red and white, and the ensign
of the arms of the United States in dark blue on a white field, the
flag signaled ship captains that this vessel had legal sanction to
stop and board. The symbol of law enforcement authority.

The Coast Guard boat came alongside the cargo ship. Several
men in crisp white uniforms came aboard.

Yao squelched his rising panic. He had come so far in this
audacious plan. He couldn't fail now. His country needed this man
and his knowledge. Marc Wayne was the vital key to getting the
Meissner Effect Generator functional. With this technology, Yao
envisioned his country becoming rich and powerful, strong, and
admired. He had to make this work. Falling back on his training,
Yao inhaled deeply, grounded himself in the moment, and focused
his attention on his options.

Chapter Fifty-six

Gennett's radio operator arrived with a report. The ship his men were inspecting was owned by a Shanghai based electronics firm called DHU Aerocomposites. Interestingly, Boeing owned 30 percent of the Chinese company.

The official statement said that DHU had no ties to the Chinese military but manufactured aircraft parts and materials strictly for commercial use.

Right.

"Pass the word," Gennett instructed his Lieutenant Commander. "Tell the search party to be extra thorough."

Chapter Fifty-seven

The leader of the armed boarding party addressed the ship's captain as his men systematically scattered throughout the vessel. For a cargo boat this large, the opportunity remained vast to stash something away from probing eyes. To hide something as diminutive as a man.

Turning down the hallway lined with sleeping quarters, two Coast Guardsmen took opposite sides of the passageway. At the end of the row, Lt. Vince Ford entered a room and was startled to find a casket. His eyes narrowed. This would be an ideal place to hide an American reluctant to leave his homeland.

A baby-faced man, Lt. Ford approached the casket and attempted to lift the lid. The top of the box refused to reveal the contents inside.

"Perhaps I can help." The voice came from behind him.

Turning, Lt. Ford saw a Chinese man, slightly gray at the temples. "I want to see inside this casket."

"Certainly." The Chinese man made a slight bow in the direction of the casket. "The casket belongs to a relative of one of the owners of our company. He traveled to the United States in the vain hope of finding a cure for his disease."

"Disease?"

The older man lowered his voice. "A humiliating condition that caused the flesh to rot from his bones."

Lt. Ford felt his belly turn. "Who are you?"

The Chinese man indicated the coffin. "The casket, as you

experienced, has been sealed to prevent not only dishonor to the dead but to prevent the contagious disease from affecting another."

Ford swallowed. "I have to see inside this casket."

"As you wish." He reached into his breast pocket and produced a paper. "According to your laws, here is the death certificate."

The lieutenant studied the document carefully and found everything in order. He handed back the paper and focused once more on the distasteful task at hand.

"You must wear a mask to open the casket," came a second voice, this one with a Chinese accent. Lt. Ford looked up to see a second man enter the small quarters.

"I am the ship's doctor." He handed a medical mask and rubber gloves to the Coast Guardsman. "In addition to the unpleasant appearance and the contagiousness of the disease, you will notice the odor of decay as you get near the body. Though the honorable relative has been properly preserved, the body was not discovered immediately after the demise."

Clenching his teeth, the lieutenant accepted the mask and rubber gloves. As predicted, when he bent close to the casket, the stench made his stomach threaten to turn inside out.

"I can get you a scalpel—a surgical knife to cut through the seal," the ship's doctor offered.

The lieutenant stepped back, blinked, and nodded. "Yes. That would be helpful."

The doctor disappeared. A second later, his Coast Guard teammate poked his head inside the room. "All clear on my side. You ready to move on?"

The lieutenant leaned forward once more and cautiously inhaled. The smell caused him to retch. He stepped back and pulled the mask from his face. "Yeah. I'm done here." He peeled the gloves from his hands and pressed them into the older Chinese man's hands as he quickly exited the room to follow his teammate.

Chapter Fifty-eight

Mere days after her flight to Indiana, Mallory sat aboard another plane. This time, the aircraft navigated east. She had been excited to land in Indiana and have a few days with family and friends. Now she reversed the trip, feeling as burdened as the treasury under the national debt.

Beside a miniature package of pretzels on her tray table, the stewardess had left a plastic cup with soda. Mallory didn't remember ordering the drink. Ignored, the ice had melted.

Was she really cut out to be in a predominantly male industry? That she would remain in her position until she located Marc went without question. Surrounded by the resources and experts in the agency, she had the best chance of tracking his journey and retrieving her brother. But then what? After such a colossal bumble, she couldn't stay at the FBI. Certainly, everyone had assignments that went awry. Recently, Mallory had read the autobiography of the commander of the US military's Delta Force. Several of their missions failed before they had success.

But this situation reached far beyond a plan that had not gone according to specifications. Marc had become entangled like a bear in a bramble patch. Her exuberance had endangered a United States citizen she had sworn to protect. Worse, she alone held responsibility for her brother being in an explosive circumstance while she struggled to dig up the confidence to assure herself that he would survive. Would he? What had she gotten him into?

She turned her face to the window so no one would see the

tears she fought.

Where else could she use her research skills? She didn't ever again want to be in a setting where she risked the lives of those she loved. What had she been thinking? If Marc became harmed as a result of her, how could she survive? The guilt of the present situation already left her breathless, as if a horse stood parked on her chest.

The FBI had appealed to her because she could be part of a dedicated team that served as a watchdog, a protection for the United States of America. Mallory's parents had been deeply patriotic. Her childhood heroes were Patrick Henry and Joshua Chamberlain. Like those two men, Mallory longed to be involved in significant work for the unique liberty of her country.

Rather than championing freedom, she had successfully stripped Marc of his. She closed the window shade, so she no longer saw her reflection. Someone had Marc and would force him to make his patent a functioning reality. What motivation would his captors use to secure his cooperation? She shuddered to consider some of the torturous methods she had heard people use to pry what they wanted from another. There were some aspects of her line of work that weren't pleasant. She had been stunned to learn the depth of deprivation, the level of evil human beings were capable of. She chided herself for ignoring that information when she concocted her strategy to plug the leak from the Patent Office.

And Marc's patent for the Meissner Effect Device was just a theory. Even if he decided to cooperate, how could Marc build something that was not possible?

He couldn't.

She had to find him.

Chapter Fifty-nine

Several hours later, the Colonel allowed himself to finally relax his defenses. The Coast Guard ship had gone on her way without incident. An hour later, the captain's errand boy had returned to inform Yao that they were safely in international waters and beyond probing eyes.

The ship's doctor had helped return Marc to a narrow bunk in the room next to Yao's own where the inventor would stay in a medically induced slumber for the rest of the journey. A helicopter would meet them soon and expedite their arrival to the laboratory.

"Here, this will help, though not much." The doctor had handed him a surgical mask. Yao secured the mask over his face, but the smell that wafted into the room after the doctor opened the casket made a man swear off eating for life.

With medical tongs, the doctor lifted from the casket a kidney-shaped dish that held a diseased appendix. Quickly, he dumped the offensive item into a bag and sealed the biohazard closed. He opened the cabin door and handed the bag to a waiting ensign. "Dispose of this properly."

"Do I want to know what that was?" The Colonel opened the window to allow the sea air to cleanse the room.

"Just after we left port, a sailor, who had complained of abdominal pain for days, collapsed. I knew what the problem was from an earlier exam, but the boy wouldn't believe he needed surgery. Lucky for you, I had not had time to dispose of the infected organ when you summoned me again. The appendix had putrefied within his body. Your orders were to make the casket unopenable."

Yao removed his mask and inhaled the biting salty air. "Commendable, doctor."

The ship's doctor bowed slightly and turned his attention to the care of the sleeping patient.

Now, just before he retired for the night, Yao savored a shot of tequila. The first shot he drank in celebration for making the journey successfully this far. The second and third shots were to calm his nerves enough to let him sleep.

Chapter Sixty

In the conference room, Mallory paced behind the chair where she usually sat. Her mind ricocheted from imagining Marc's fate to doing the job she trained to do. As a research specialist, she should have found plenty of leads by now.

Thomas stirred two creams into a cup and handed the coffee to his co-worker. She ignored his offer.

"Where has Helen of Troy been carried off to?" Already talking, Deverell blew into the room. "Thomas, what do we have to date?"

"The patent application for the Meissner Effect Device was leaked from the USPTO. We know who was the mole in the Patent Office."

Mallory circled the room. "Now he's dead."

"That's a dead end."

"That's a bad pun," Mallory said.

"Sorry." Deverell tossed a wadded gum wrapper toward the trash can. The rim shot bounced back onto the floor. "That means the foreign entity will try to cultivate a new contact."

"We have a team working on that." Thomas set Mallory's cup at her empty place and took a seat.

"Anyone with anything worthy of blackmail is a target." Deverell watched Mallory pace. "What else?"

"We suspect that whoever has received the patent information is having trouble getting the invention to work because our inventor has disappeared."

"Kidnapped," Mallory snapped.

Thomas rubbed the top of his head. "Kidnapped," he echoed softly.

"We don't know where to begin looking." Mallory faced her boss. She considered this meeting a colossal waste of time that could be invested in finding leads. The sooner she could get out of here, the faster she could be back to following the one sure thing she knew; Marc had been flown to Southern California and one of the men with him was probably Chinese.

"Based on the results of previous leaks from the Patent Office," Deverell met her gaze, "the patent and our inventor are probably in Asia."

"Great." Mallory threw up her hands. "That narrows it down to a mere quarter of the globe."

Thomas crossed to the map on the wall. "Since the cutting-edge jet engine was developed in China, why not begin there?"

"I'll get right on it."

"Whoa." Deverell put a restraining hand on Mallory's arm. "Before you invade the People's Republic, while China developed the engine, based on our information, I don't credit them with the ability to directly acquire top secret material."

Mallory folded her arms. "Then where do we begin?"

"If China is the recipient of the information, they probably received the designs from another entity. Someone that pilfers marketable secrets."

"A governmental entity or private entrepreneur?"

"That's the question. Where is Cinderella's slipper hidden? Has Marc been delivered to the highest bidder, or is he making the Meissner Device operational for the marketers?"

"Unless." Thomas leaned forward. "We can coax them into showing us where they are."

"How?" Thomas had Mallory's full attention.

"They are probably working around the clock to get this Holy

Grail up and running to position themselves ahead of the rest of the world in military superiority."

"Go on." Deverell loaded a second piece of gum into his mouth.

"What if they believe we are also perfecting the design?" Thomas looked from Mallory to Deverell. "What if we make circumstances look like we got the invention running first?"

Feeling taut as a harp string, Mallory resumed pacing. "How will that lead us to Marc?"

"We make it look like we completed the invention, but it's faulty. Then see who is the most interested." Thomas became animated as the idea developed. "They will be the only other entity besides us who knows about the Meissner Device patent."

Mallory placed her palms on the table and leaned toward her boss. "How do we keep them from killing Marc?"

Mouth open, Deverell chomped loudly on his gum. "They won't hurt him as long as he is valuable to them. Until we find him, we make them believe he is irreplaceable."

Thomas made notes on the paper in front of him. "We leak information that the device had a problem. A deadly problem, but the answer was found in a small-town inventor's workshop."

Mallory smiled for the first time in days. "That makes Marc too pivotal to dispose of."

"A Trojan horse." Deverell pointed his pen in Thomas's direction. "We also leak that now the apparatus is working, and that the small-town inventor has mysteriously disappeared."

Chapter Sixty-one

Coming awake, Marc felt reluctant to leave the deep slumber. The dreamy sensation of complete relaxation seductively enticed him to stay like a warm bed on a frigid Saturday morning.

Opening his eyes, he looked around from the single bed where he lay. In the sparse room, morning light glowed through narrow windows positioned far above a man's head. Too high to see outside. Opposite the bed, he noticed a single door. The only other furniture was a chair and table holding a folded set of clothes, a bottle of water, and two covered dishes.

Where was he? How did he get here? Why was he here? Nothing made sense. There wasn't anything familiar about this place.

Gingerly, Marc stretched and sat up. His head swam, and he felt as weak as one of Dr. Thurmond's newborn kittens. His body ached, and his stomach grumbled with hunger. The floor felt cold under his bare feet, and the folding metal chair drawn up to the table was unyielding. Lifting the lids, Marc found a bowl heaped with warm rice. The second dish held mystery meat in a dark sauce. He sniffed. This smelled nothing like the rich Chinese dishes Nancy brought him at the steak and Chinese food restaurant back home.

Greedily, Marc downed half the water and set to work on the food. With his belly full, he felt stronger. Surveying his surroundings, he tried the door. Locked. Stacking the table on the bed and the chair on top of the table, he stood on tiptoe, but the window occupied a place too high in the wall.

Frustrated, Marc took the clothes to the corner nook that served as a bathroom. A nozzle spit enough water for a shower, and he gladly washed off the smell of having gone too long without washing. His beard indicated that enough time had passed to give him that unshaved look that Hollywood actors sported. And his facial hair grew slowly.

He stood the metal bed frame on end in another attempt to see outside when the door opened. Flanked by two armed soldiers, a man entered. His bearing identified him as someone in authority. Recognizing the uniforms, Marc's knees threatened to buckle.

Chinese.

Was the Chinese military on United States soil? His brain raced to recall what nearby countries were friendly with China.

Or could it be possible that Marc and this place were on the other side of the globe?

Chapter Sixty-two

Seeking any clue to Marc's captors and his whereabouts, Mallory read through the reports sent in from the Coast Guard, airports, and border patrol. Hearing a light knock on her office door, she looked up. Thomas stood in the open doorway. She spied the Styrofoam cup in his hand, steam rising through the small hole in the lid.

She shook her head. "Thanks, Thomas, but coffee is—"

"Tearing up your stomach." He stepped to her desk. "I know. The condition probably has something to do with worry. Psychological stress is a contributing factor in the formation of duodenal ulcers or peptic ulcers. This is a small erosion—"

"Hole."

"Or hole in the gastrointestinal tract. Common duodenal ulcers occur in the first 12 inches of the small intestine beyond the stomach."

Mallory leaned her elbows on her desk. "All right, Encyclopedia Thomas. How do you know so much about ulcers?"

"In fact, I know a great deal about a great deal of topics."

"Fess up."

"Been there, done that." He set the cup under her nose where chocolate-scented steam tickled her nostrils. "Which is why I brought you a soothing hot cocoa."

"Thanks."

He indicated the paperwork scattered in loose piles on her desk and the open reports on her computer screen. "Find anything interesting?"

"Not yet. Wanna add your unjaded eye to the hunt?"

"Thought you'd never ask." He plopped down, shuffled loose papers into a heap, and began sorting the pile.

"Why are you so eager to help me?"

Not bothering to look up, he continued to scan the reports. "What's on my to-do list today is not half as interesting."

"And?"

He was quiet for a moment. When he met her eyes, she saw worry there. "And I'm concerned about Marc."

Chapter Sixty-three

The Chinese man regarded Marc, his gaze measuring, weighing, considering. A slight gesture of his hand sent one of the soldiers to return the bed to the original horizontal position.

"Sit."

Marc didn't move.

The soldier moved to enforce the command, but a single syllable stopped him. A word Marc didn't recognize. Chinese.

"Who are you?" Marc saw the soldiers stand ready for any instruction from this man. They would do his bidding. They were also uniformed, armed, and obviously militarily trained. Weighing the options, Marc decided at this moment their physical abilities trumped his brains.

"You are here to complete your invention." Shorter than Marc, and older, the man spoke as if the command were a perfectly reasonable demand.

"Where is here?"

"This is a research and development facility." He spoke without an accent.

Marc held his voice level. "Where am I?"

"You will remain here, as our guest, of course, until the device is functional." The statement sounded authoritative.

"What device?"

"The Meissner Device."

Marc swallowed and sat down on the bed. Like tumblers in a combination lock, disjointed impressions quickly fit together.

Mallory's request for a tempting patent application, the disconcerting visit from Mr. Spencer, and the strange dream state he had floated in before waking up in this bizarre setting. The people his sister sought didn't play nice.

He quickly bit back a nervous urge to either laugh or rapidly explain that the situation had escalated into a gigantic misunderstanding. *You've got me confused with someone who you really should have kidnapped and dragged to your evil lair in who-knows-where. The Meissner Device is still theoretical. Not yet even a laboratory curiosity. Admittedly close, but not close enough to warrant this type of subterfuge.*

Marc raked his hands through his hair. Yeah, they would be fine with that explanation. Fall all over each other apologizing for the silly mistake and book him a first-class seat on a non-stop jet back to Indiana. With real china and linen napkins as opposed to the great treatment he had experienced in the process of arriving here. Where was here, anyhow?

"You begin to understand." The man in authority pulled near the metal chair and sat opposite Marc, staring at him.

They drugged and dumped me in this upscale place—he glanced at the dingy room and ancient necessities—*the inventor they needed. Certainly, the guy who can't get the Meissner Device functional, or happens to mention that the idea is presently impossible, will quickly and painfully disappear. I'm allergic to pain. And I'm not ready to disappear.*

"I understand all right." Marc showed the man his middle finger.

Again, the soldier with the short fuse moved to strike Marc, but the man halted him with a word.

"The international means of communication." Marc smirked at the soldier who plainly wanted to rip Marc's face from his head. "Now you and your baboons understand *me*."

The man put his hands on his knees and leaned forward. "I

will be plain. You will get the Meissner Device operational. Quickly. If you cannot, you are of no use to me. No one knows where you are. There will be no, as you call it, cavalry to the rescue. If you cannot complete the device, I have no need of you." He allowed his words to stand between them. "Do you understand?"

Marc held up both middle fingers.

The man stood to leave. A soldier opened the door, and the man turned back to Marc. "I will give you a little time to reconsider your situation. But not long."

The men left, pulling the door closed behind them. Marc heard the hollow sound of the lock on the outside slide into place.

Chapter Sixty-four

For the next two days, Marc remained alone. Completely alone. No visitors. No food. The water to his small bath area was shut off, and the toilet he used smelled. The only consolation, if one could be found in this dire situation, was that he became dehydrated and no longer used the toilet.

Marc had gone over the room, searching for any means of escape. Above his reach hung a video camera. Someone kept an eye on him.

Frustrated, he dropped onto the bed. His hands laced behind his head, he mentally searched for options. Again. Marc had concluded he must be in another country. Someone had gone to a lot of trouble to get him here. Who would want the Meissner Device enough to risk an international incident? Who would benefit to the degree that they would kidnap him? None of the answers he came to boded well for him or Mallory or world peace.

Hearing someone at the door, he quickly came to his feet.

As before, two soldiers flanked the man whose uniform identified him as a Colonel. "Have you decided to cooperate?"

"Have you decided to return me to my home?"

"As soon as the Meissner Device is functional."

Marc shook his head. "Not happening."

The Colonel beckoned a fourth man into the room. Small and soft, he carried a nylon medical bag. A myriad of possibilities ran through Marc's mind, and none of them gave him confidence. At a nod from their superior, the soldiers grabbed Marc's arms and pushed him toward the bed. Marc fought like a cat on the way to a bath. His pulse furious, and sweaty from the exertion, Marc flailed against being forced onto the thin mattress and pinned there.

The Colonel leaned close, so their eyes met. "I will have the Meissner Device. You will make it operational."

Kicking and thrashing, Marc glared back. From the black bag, the fourth man removed a syringe which he filled with the contents from a small bottle.

"Succinylcholine." The Colonel narrated the movements of the man with the needle. "An effective paralytic. Administered intramuscularly, the substance immediately depolarizes the muscles while leaving them flaccid."

He nodded, and the man with the loaded syringe approached. "Immediately you will experience fasciculation. Like a brief seizure. Then you will be completely paralyzed, unable to even breathe for yourself."

Like the sudden fall through the pond ice back home, shocking fear washed over Marc. With the panic of a drowning man, he renewed his struggle against the powerful arms that held him.

"No," he yelled as the sting of the needle pierced his arm. Just as the Colonel predicted, Marc experienced a sudden and violent twitch that began at his head and rapidly swept to his feet. Immediately, Marc lost feeling in his body. Even his lungs forgot to breathe. Within seconds, his body exhaled. No matter how hard Marc concentrated, in his drugged state, he could not force himself to inhale again. Complete powerlessness and dark hopelessness descended. Alarm surged through his awareness like a tsunami as the unfamiliar face who had injected him bent near and fitted a breathing bag over Marc's face.

The Colonel moved into his now paralyzed and narrow line of vision. "Not one muscle of your body can move. Your diaphragm no longer pulls life-giving oxygen into your lungs." The Colonel worked the breathing bag. Mercifully, air entered and exited Marc's body.

"This is me breathing for you." The Colonel's voice echoed sinisterly in his ear.

Marc counted. Every five seconds, the man in control granted air. For a full minute, the Colonel breathed for him a dozen times.

"And this is me not breathing for you." The breathing bag stopped its function and lay like a deflated balloon against his face. All his life, Marc's lungs had done their job efficiently and effectively without any prodding from him. Yet, now he could not convince them to do the duty they had faithfully conducted since before his birth. His body lay still but far from peaceful. Fear and terror warred within while he fought to remain calm and consider his options. His heartbeat thundered in his ears. Deprived of oxygen, electric dots of light and color danced in his vision, obscuring the cruel and determined face of his oppressor.

Mallory and Violet. Would he see them again? Would he have a chance to return to his quiet Midwest hometown and the life of inventing, writing patents, and guest teaching that he had created for himself? With occasional visits to DC to see Mallory's world, punctuated by her trips back home. Did Hebron get Marc's message about supplemental uses of his invention? Would Thurmond Yoder miss their morning conversation?

"The doctor has administered a paralyzing drug." The Colonel moved into Marc's limited vision. "A common prescription for those in serious medical situations."

Even as he dropped into an oxygen-deprived unconsciousness, air pushed into Marc's lungs and his chest inflated. After three breaths, Marc could see the Colonel clearly.

"This is me breathing for you again. Your life depends on me. And I will keep you alive to give me what I need." He pressed the bag to send fresh oxygen into Marc's lungs. Releasing the pressure, the bag received the exhaled air. Slowly, the process repeated. This time much slower. Marc's lungs were hungry for air.

With calculated slowness, the Colonel dispensed stingy measurements. He leaned closer. "Now we have an understanding, and I will return your body to you."

The bag continued to provide air for the next minute as the drug released control, and Marc's lungs gradually returned to doing their task. Free from the breathing bag, Marc sucked in a great amount of air, feeling his traumatized body inflate. He felt like a bulldozer had rolled over him.

Roughly, the two soldiers dragged the Gumby-leg prisoner from the bed and dropped him into the chair at the crude table. In front of Marc sat a computer. On the screen streamed a picture.

"Look closely." The Colonel's voice spoke into his ear. Too near. The man gave Marc the creeps, and he fought an urge to bat him away like an Indiana mosquito on a summer evening. In truth, Marc didn't think he had the strength.

Marc squinted in an attempt to focus. His eyes struggled to recover from the recent lack of necessary air. The fuzzy image that danced before his vision began to clear. But what he saw made no sense.

Chapter Sixty-five

When several hours of search returned no results, Mallory pressed her palms against her temples.

Thomas stood to stretch. "According to the timeline, our window for clues would be in the first three days of his disappearance."

Watching him pace across her office, Mallory stifled a yawn. "We are relatively sure he was removed from the area via ambulance." She reviewed her list of facts scribbled on a pad of paper.

"And we tracked the medical flight leaving Fort Wayne's Smith Field the same day bound for the West Coast. The co-pilot identified Marc's hair."

"The next step," Mallory pushed back from her desk, "would be a flight or ship. Unless they used a train."

"A train would mean he's probably still in the United States." Thomas considered the map pinned to the wall. He placed one pushpin to mark Dixon, Indiana.

Mallory secured a second pin to mark the Santa Ana airport in Southern California where the pilot said they had delivered their passengers. "Mexico?"

Thomas eyed the distance. "Someone could cross the border into Baja California by car in under two hours from the John Wayne airport."

"Or Canada?" She shook her head. "North would require another flight, and Southern California isn't strategic as a connection above the Pacific Northwest."

"Private plane?" Thomas crossed his arms. "Would they utilize another pilot?"

"Or private boat?"

"Possible." He made another track across her office. "Let's read our reports aloud. What one of us is not noticing, perhaps the other will."

Mallory scrolled back to the top of her computer screen and read through the entries aloud. When that report yielded no results, Thomas picked up a page from his stack and read to Mallory. A long list of airplanes and ships had been searched.

"Coast Guard boarded and searched a Chinese cargo ship named Shanghai Sumi owned by DHU Aerocomposites."

"Wait." Thomas stood behind her chair to read over her shoulder. "We've had dealings with them before. Let me use your computer."

Mallory gave him her seat, and he began typing. "Here it is."

Hope warred with desperation as Mallory yearned for a direction to search for her brother.

"DHU Aerocomposites is owned by three entities. Boeing owns 30 percent, and Franklin Fabrics owns 30 percent."

"I know Boeing." Mallory studied the screen over Thomas's shoulder. "And Franklin Fabrics is a US based firm with offices worldwide."

He murmured a list. "Franklin Fabrics manufactures structural fiber, reinforced fabrics, honeycombed cores, aircraft structures, and composite and complex glues that are vital to aircraft construction."

She tapped her foot nervously. "Who is the third owner?"

"DHU Aerocomposites. An Asian company that manufactures commercial airlines."

"Okay." Mallory wrote the three entities on her notes. "What are you thinking?"

"Spokesmen for both Boeing and Franklin Fabrics said that its use of aircraft parts and materials were strictly for commercial and civilian ends." Thomas opened another window and clicked on a link. "During investigations, they stated that they were fully confident that DHU had no ties to the Chinese military."

"Why were they investigated?"

Thomas rubbed the back of his neck. "As I recall, private studies uncovered several links with the Chinese military establishment involving DHU."

"What kind of links?"

"Let me access my notes." He typed in security codes to bring up his files. While he searched, Mallory paced, the forgotten hot chocolate in her hand.

"Here it is," he said finally. "According to State Department reports, the Chinese government entity that owns a minority share of DHU, also produces fighters, nuclear-capable bombers, and aviation weapons systems for the People's Liberation Army."

Mallory faced him. "And their cargo ship left a Chinese-owned dock space in Long Beach during our target time period."

Thomas sighed. "But the Coast Guard searched the ship and found nothing."

"Nothing." Mallory swore. "I need a lead. A concrete lead, Thomas, not another dead end."

Chapter Sixty-six

On the sparse table, the computer blinked and glowed. Connected to a telecommunications application that provided video chats between electronic devices, an image appeared without sound.

The picture pulled at Marc's heart. Through the video camera, Marc viewed his own living room in the home where he had grown up. As a kid, Marc spent evenings in this place with his family. His dad smoked a pipe that smelled like roasted cherries while his mom read aloud. Marc and his sister sprawled in front of the fireplace. Dipping into a small bottle of color with a smell that stung his nostrils, Mallory painted her nails. While most boys his age built with Legos, Marc tinkered with erector sets, switches, pulleys, and batteries. Some nights they played the family's favorite game, *Trivial Pursuit*.

Peering closer to the screen, he experienced a wash of homesickness. He longed to be back in Indiana, and not in this filthy cell with powerful strangers threatening his life. Would he ever be able to return to his previous life? Did anyone return from a situation like he found himself in now?

"Do you recognize the room?" Like a bully on the playground dangling Marc's new puppy over his head, the Colonel's taunt sounded cruel.

"It's my house." Marc swung on them in a rage. "Get out of my house! Get out of my life!" He charged the Colonel who stepped back, and the soldiers instantly filled the space between the two, quickly reigning in the furious captive. The two burly men overcame Marc and held him stretched between them. Calmly, the Colonel swung a fist into Marc's stomach, tearing the air from his lungs. Already weak, Marc had little strength to fight or resist as the Colonel pummeled him with blow after blow until Marc hung limp.

At a nod from their superior, the soldiers dropped Marc once more into the folding metal chair in front of the computer screen. Bent in half and gasping for breath, Marc crossed his arms protectively over his bruised and beaten belly.

"Watch closely." The Colonel spoke Chinese into a satellite phone. In moments, Marc watched in horror as three men dragged a woman to the couch and pinned her down. Though it was difficult to see her face in the commotion, the size looked familiar. Straining to be sure, and frantic that this horror not be true, he recognized her hair. The color of cinnamon. Mallory.

Deep, primal anger mixed with fear caught in Marc's throat and surged through his body. And the Colonel anticipated his reaction. As Marc came off his seat, the soldiers pressed him down. Like a spider with her prey, the Colonel spun a wide roll of duct tape around the captive and the chair. With more strength than he knew he possessed, Marc fought his captors. Dreadfully out-numbered and out-muscled, he struggled hopelessly against forces he could not budge.

"Monster!" Teeth tightly clenched, Marc yelled, "Let her go!"

His voice oily with confidence, the Colonel ordered, "Watch." Digging fingers into his chin, he held Marc's face to the screen.

"Call off your buffoons!" Marc's panic spun out of control. "Don't let them touch her!"

The Colonel chuckled. "No one is going to rape her. Though it was difficult to prevent even such loyal men from enjoying the few privileges of their job." He sighed theatrically. "No, she won't be raped. Not this time." He squeezed Marc's shoulder. "Though that could be arranged. Consider this mercy a trade for your cooperation."

With renewed vigor, Marc struggled futilely against his bonds.

The Colonel spoke into the cell phone while Marc watched the screen. He needed to protect his sister. Bile rose in his throat as three men held Mallory on the couch. Moving close to the camera, a fourth man held a syringe in one hand and a small, rubber-topped bottle in the other.

"Perhaps you recognize the bottle and syringe?" The Colonel let the words hang between them.

"Don't." Marc shuddered as he recalled the nightmare he had just experienced with the drug. "Please."

"Succinylcholine." The Colonel narrated. "An effective paralytic. Administered intramuscularly, the drug immediately depolarizes the muscles while leaving them flaccid."

From somewhere far from his home in Indiana, Marc watched helplessly as the needle pierced Mallory's arm.

"You son of a…" Marc watched the men who had held Mallory move back.

"Immediately she will experience fasciculation. Like a brief seizure. Then she will be completely paralyzed, unable to even breathe for herself."

Beginning at his sister's head, a rapid seizure-like movement quaked through her body. Then she stopped breathing.

"Not one muscle of her body can move." The Colonel narrated in a calm, informative tone as if he described the ordinary removal of a splinter. "Her diaphragm no longer pulls necessary oxygen into her pretty lungs."

The Colonel spoke into the phone.

Marc snarled. "You unfeeling beast."

The man who had administered the deadly injection

positioned a breathing bag over her face, but Marc's relief felt tenuous. Mercifully, air entered and exited his sister's body. And cruelly, the life-giving oxygen could be taken from her in an instant.

"This is me breathing for her." The Colonel whispered the words in his ear.

Marc counted. Every five seconds, her chest rose with the oxygen delivered to her. For a full minute, the man who held the bag breathed for his sister.

"And this is me not breathing for her." The Colonel spoke into the phone. On the screen, a wiry man with dark hair pressed a cell phone to his ear and then said something Marc could not hear to the one who held the breathing bag. The bag stopped the simple yet vital function and lay like a deflated balloon against his sister's face.

"A human typically experiences brain damage when deprived of air for longer than four minutes."

"Don't hurt her," Marc pleaded.

"Now that I have your attention, let's talk about your cooperation."

"Give her air, for God's sake!"

"I will provide what she needs when you give me what I require." He pointed to the time at the top right of the computer screen. "She has been without oxygen for a full minute."

He stood erect, clasping his hands behind his back as if giving a college course lecture. "Hypoxia or hypoxiation is a pathological condition in which the body as a whole is deprived of an adequate supply of oxygen. The brain in your sister's lovely head will suffer cerebral anoxia. Complete lack of oxygen. Initially, the body responds to lowered blood oxygen by redirecting blood to the brain and increasing vital cerebral blood flow. However, if circulation cannot be increased or if doubled blood flow does not correct the problem, symptoms of cerebral hypoxia will begin to appear."

"Stop it!" Marc fought against his bonds.

His captor went on as if he didn't hear. "Mild symptoms include difficulties with complex learning tasks and reductions in short-term memory. If oxygen deprivation continues, cognitive disturbances and decreased motor control will result. The skin becomes bluish—termed cyanosis—and heart rate increases. Continued oxygen deprivation as is happening here," he pointed to the screen, "results in coma, seizures, cessation of brain stem reflexes, and," he paused to allow Marc to mentally take the next step, "brain death."

Still unemotional, the Colonel indicated the time on the screen. "It has been two full minutes. As you have experienced, these physical malfunctions set in quickly."

Hungrily, Marc's eyes bore into the 12-inch screen for any hint that his sister might really be all right. That this wicked nightmare would end, and he would wake any moment. His inventive mind searched for solutions, for some way to oppose these bullies, save Mallory, and refuse the Meissner Device to these men. The device was only theoretical, anyway. Even if he agreed to cooperate, it would be a hoax. If they were willing to suffocate Mallory in front of him, what were they capable of doing when they realized he couldn't make the weapon of their ambitions functional? Yet, he could not allow Mallory to die. Not because he refused to bend.

"Okay!" The word burst from Marc's lips, and he realized he had been holding his breath. "Give her air!"

"Have we reached an understanding?" He slowly drug out the words.

"Yes!" Marc slumped. "Yes, whatever you want. Just let her live."

The Colonel spoke into the cell phone. The airbag remained motionless on Mallory's face.

"Hurry!" Marc heard the anxiety and desperation in his own

voice and didn't care.

"Be patient." The Colonel waved the cell phone. "It takes a moment for the signal to reach the satellite orbiting in space and then transfer to the cell phone somewhere in your house in Indiana."

When Marc thought he would explode with panic, at last he saw movement on the screen. The dark-haired man, who reminded Marc of an insect, put the cell phone to his ear and then spoke quickly to his partner. The air bag inflated. Mallory's chest rose and fell once more with vital oxygen.

Of course, Marc knew he would give in as soon as he recognized the danger surrounding his sister. He had no idea how he would hide the fact that the Meissner Device was merely theoretical. For now, he had bought time. Time for himself. Time for Mallory.

The Colonel turned off the computer.

"Hey! Turn it on. How do I know she's all right?"

His nemesis crossed his arms across his chest. "She is fine. The drug will wear off in about two minutes."

"And? How do I know she is safe from you and your pet rottweilers?"

"She is safe as long as you give me—"

"The Meissner Device." Marc filled in the rest of the sentence. "I got that part."

"Excellent." He waved toward the guard who cut Marc's duct tape bonds. "I will show you where you will assemble your invention."

Chapter Sixty-seven

Marc felt miserable. How in the world would he get out of here? He had to get to Mallory. Where were they holding her? How were they treating her? What were her co-workers, Logan Deverell and Thomas Ridley, doing to locate her? He had to find a way to get her away from this power-driven bully and his murderous goons.

While more than merely theoretical, the Meissner Device remained only partially designed. Even if he could get the idea up and running, did he want to do that for these people? He doubted they planned to use the technology for the good of mankind. Kidnapping him had been his first clue. Now they held Mallory's life suspended over his head like an egg about to drop from the Washington Monument.

They could have just invited him. They could have asked. They could have held a worldwide symposium on travel and propulsion options. They could have done a million other approaches. Kidnapping lay at the rock bottom of the list. The Colonel was desperate. Or maniacal.

And if Marc did make the Meissner Device functional, did he believe for one minute that his captors would pat his head with approval and happily send him back home? Release Mallory so the two could have a family reunion back in the United States? Could he ever return to his comfortable office in the Midwest next door to Dr. Thurmond? Back to his routine mornings biking to the office, developing inventions, and waiting for Violet to arrive smelling of spring lavender? Hearing her putter in the kitchen where she brewed the honest Earl Grey tea perfectly laced with honey and cream. The day began with her smile.

These were the questions that kept him awake at night. He had tried a hundred different scenarios, but now, as he tinkered with his design, he let the reality of the situation settle over him. His life was forever altered. The immediate question needed an answer; could he find a way to keep himself and his sister alive?

He glanced around the spacious lab, surprisingly modern in this ancient building. At various workstations, white-coated lab workers concentrated on projects. Most worked on various aspects of the Meissner Device. Using his patent information. How the heck did these people get his application?

Certainly, this lab served as the landing spot for the patents stolen from the United States Patent and Trademark Office. Marc stood in the center of the thievery Mallory and her team were attempting to trace and shut down. When he got the Meissner Device Generator working, the Colonel would no longer have use for him. Or for Mallory. Especially not Mallory with her connections to the FBI. Nor would he send Marc home. When the device became operational, Marc's captors would keep him here to continue to make new developments. Or, more likely, they would kill him. He would be the disposable crewmember.

He swore under his breath.

"Excuse me?" The voice sounded close.

Marc looked over. He'd been so absorbed in his thoughts he had not noticed the young woman working nearby.

"Did you say something?"

Good English with a Chinese accent, he observed. He shook his head. "Just thinking out loud."

She tipped her head and studied him. "I know you," she said softly.

"Haven't I seen you someplace before?" His falsetto dripped

with sarcasm.

Nonplussed, she nodded. "You spoke at my university."

"Trust me, I've never been here before." He felt in no mood for anything other than his own self-pity. "Wherever *here* is."

She gazed at him levelly. "I studied electro-physics in the United States."

He couldn't keep the edge from his voice. "Nice to see you are putting your education to good use."

She looked puzzled, and then frowned. Tossing her shoulder length hair in the same way Mallory did when she was agitated, the girl moved away.

The following day, Marc still grappled for a solution to his situation when he noticed the scientist in charge hurry to the large doors. Colonel Yao had just made one of his dramatic entrances. The two had a hushed conversation, the scientist doing most of the talking in that nervous way he had only in the Colonel's presence.

The two walked through the work in process, Yao occasionally asking a question, the scientist overly explaining.

Discreetly, Marc kept an eye on Yao. There had to be a chink in the staid man's armor. Dismissing the relieved tour guide, Yao slowly circulated in the room. Coming to the girl who had talked to Marc, Yao stopped and spoke to her. Though Marc couldn't hear their words, he watched carefully.

Then the Colonel appeared at Marc's elbow. "Your progress is too slow."

Easy for you to say. All you have to do is threaten to suffocate people. Marc turned on him. "I didn't exactly bring my notes. I have to recreate years of work here—from memory. You might have thought of that when you started this parade."

"For your sake—for your sister's sake—complete the prototype."

Marc watched the man, his back ramrod straight, exit the lab. Though he tried to shrug off the Colonel's words, the memory of

Mallory just moments from suffocation haunted his dreams at night and his work during the day. He knew that was the Colonel's intent and grudgingly acknowledged the effectiveness of the ploy. Marc guessed Yao received pressure from those above him. Probably demands from his superiors. Maybe his career hung in the balance. But none of that compared with the very life and well-being of a beloved family member.

Several hours later, the Colonel returned. He set a carryall container in front of Marc. Reaching inside, Marc drew out his notebook filled with his equations. Then his laptop.

"The computer's internet capabilities have been disabled, of course."

"Of course."

The Colonel walked away. Marc looked inside the carryall once more. Curiously, Hebron Heath's diamond evaluating device lay at the bottom.

Chapter Sixty-eight

Mallory popped her head in Deverell's office. Her boss's forehead rested against his palm as he sat at his desk, obviously engrossed in a phone call.

"You gotta come see this." At last, she had something concrete in this convoluted case, and she could barely contain her excitement.

He waved her away.

"Now!"

When he ignored her, Mallory briskly walked over and hung up the phone.

"Geez Louise, are you crazy?" Deverell picked up the phone to reconnect. "What is wrong with you?"

She hung up the phone again. For the second time, someone had called her crazy in as many days. "We found something."

"Mallory, you can't—"

"I can and I did. Now c'mon."

"It can't be as important as who I was speaking to."

"I don't care if you were talking to the President."

"As a matter of fact—"

She grabbed his elbow, hauled him from his seat, and pushed him out of his office toward the conference room.

Rounding the corner, she found Thomas already there. "We've been studying everything that has gone across Saad's desk, combing through the mail and his phone records."

Deverell threw up his hands in surrender and dropped into a

high-backed chair at the head of the oval table. "What do you have for me, people?"

"The most interesting discovery showed up in the computer's history." Mallory snatched the remote from the tabletop and clicked in the direction of the screen. A picture of a kitten appeared.

Deverell plucked a pen from his shirt pocket and bounced the end against the table, clicking the point in and out, in and out. "Looks like a Hallmark card of Puss In Boots."

"Exactly what we thought at first glance." Thomas nodded to Mallory.

Deverell swung his chair to face the two. "So, somebody sent the guy an email greeting card."

"Look closely." Mallory pressed a button on the remote and the picture magnified. Next, she showed a second image of the same kitten. But at this magnitude, the side-by-side pictures of the same kitten looked different.

"What's that background noise, those extra strokes to the design?" Deverell leaned forward to better study the examples. "Extra pixels that don't quite belong."

"It's noise, all right." Mallory walked toward the screen, swiping the pen from Deverell's hand mid-click. "The difference between the two pictures is the information."

Deverell stood and approached the screen. "Get Jimmy up here right away from digital forensics. He needs to see this."

Thomas winked at Mallory. "Jimmy is on his way."

"What are we looking at, exactly?"

"That is a method of espionage," the voice came from the doorway, "called steganography."

They turned to see Jimmy. He stood just inside the conference room, his gaze locked on the images.

"Steganography?" Deverell repeated the new term. "It's Greek to me."

"It is Greek, actually." Jimmy pushed his John Lennon glasses higher on the bridge of his nose.

"Greek for covered writing," Mallory noted.

"Using innocuous documents, usually an image file like this cat," Jimmy carried his constant cup of chai tea, "steganography encodes the message while at the same time, concealing the fact that a message is being sent at all."

"Put it in English, Jimmy." Deverell squinted at the side-by-side pictures. "Where has the pussycat been and what did she do there?"

Jimmy dropped into one of the conference room chairs. "Greek generals tattooed sensitive information onto the shaved heads of messengers. Once their hair grew back, the messenger traveled without suspicion to the intended recipient who decrypted the message by once again shaving the messenger's head."

Deverell rubbed a meaty hand over his own thinning crown. "Nothing new under the sun."

"Indeed," Thomas agreed. "Only today, steganography makes use of email."

"For any disgruntled employee or corporate spy, this method is an ideal carrier." Mallory tossed the pen back to her boss and winced when he absently began clicking again. "Or for foreign espionage."

"Good job, you two. Now we know how important patents are being leaked." Deverell turned to Jimmy. "We need a way of disrupting this…" he waved his pen in the direction of the representation of the cat that still lit the screen.

"Steganography," Mallory filled in for him.

"This steganography."

Chapter Sixty-nine

Marc watched the Colonel approach the girl again. Part of his regular routine when he came through the laboratory, the man always made time to talk with her. Marc suspected this custom had become the most important part of the Colonel's day.

At the rear of the expansive lab, the large overhead door opened. Usually, when shipments were delivered, someone ushered Marc back to his room. Apparently, his captors were reluctant for anyone to see Marc or for Marc to see anyone beyond this carefully guarded environment.

Today, supplies were brought in from bulky military transport at anchor in the water that ran along the backside of the renovated temple. Uniformed men unloaded and a forklift busily lifted and deposited heavy loads. Marc gazed longingly at the sunshine, then away before anyone could think he seemed too interested in the outside world and escorted him back to his unfriendly cell. He positioned his body so he could observe what lay outside without appearing to do so.

Later, Marc found an excuse to go to the girl's workstation. "What university did you attend?"

This time she appeared to be the one deep in thought. She glanced up at him questioningly, so he repeated his question.

"Indiana," she stated. "Why?"

"I was trying to figure out where our paths had crossed before."

"You didn't believe me."

He shrugged. "I apologize. I was having a bad day."

She nodded and glanced nervously toward the door through which the Colonel did his usual coming and going. Marc had watched him leave not long ago after another conversation with this girl.

He put out his hand. "I'm Marc Wayne."

"I know." She ignored his hand. "You were the guest lecturer at my university."

"Please accept my apology. I was rude."

She glanced at his outstretched hand and met his gaze. "Yes, you were." She studied him before putting her small palm into his.

He gave her hand a gentle shake, suddenly aware of the comfort of a friendly touch. "And your name, physics major?"

"Lei. Lei Quong. Electro-Physics."

He turned to go and stopped. "What was the topic? Of my lecture?"

She stared at him. "You are being rude again."

As she turned away, Marc quickly stepped toward her. "Humor me. It's an honest question."

Her tone sarcastic, Lei waved her hand to encompass the large lab. "The Meissner Effect; Laboratory Oddity—"

"Or Revolutionary Tool for Mankind," he filled in, feeling like he had been punched in the stomach.

Chapter Seventy

Foreign satellites picked up a sudden beehive of activity in a formerly quiet hangar at Wright-Patterson Air Force Base in Ohio. Equipment was trucked to the location, and people were seen coming and going.

Several well-known scientists received assignments to the new project, and their invitations were purposefully sent through channels the FBI knew would be compromised by spies.

Major Orson O'Leary, a blonde, raw-boned man who chewed an unlit cigar, assumed charge of the project. "Can I choose my team?"

Deverell sat with the base commander as they briefed O'Leary. "Okay by me."

The general nodded his approval.

O'Leary wrote names. "These guys are smart thinkers and efficient." His cigar bobbed when he spoke. "With them, I can move your invention from patent to reality." He tore the page from his pad and passed the paper to Deverell.

"Good." Deverell surveyed the list. "We've equipped your laboratory. Let me know if you need additional supplies."

O'Leary moved the cigar from one side of his mouth to the other. "Simple really. I strap enough fuel to the butt of anything, it's gonna go up. Thrust and propulsion. The rest is just math to aim it where we want 'er to go. Heck, with enough flammable material, I can launch a Sherman tank into orbit. From space, we can point the muzzle directly at the North Koreans."

Deverell broke in. "This isn't a shoot 'em all and let God sort it out assignment. The Meissner Effect Device doesn't even utilize—"

With a hand on his arm, the commander cut off Deverell's speech. "Look over the plans, O'Leary. You'll know what to do."

When the cigar-chewing Irishman went out to the Humvee that waited to take him to the new laboratory, the commander clapped Deverell's shoulder. "You alphabet agency guys need to know when to shut up and let us military guys get the job done."

"But this device doesn't require any flammable fuels."

"He'll figure that out." Reaching for the list O'Leary had made, the older man looked at the short column and grunted. "Good men. They can get a beluga whale in a polka-dot tutu to fly."

Chapter Seventy-one

The Colonel wore intimidation like his uniform. Careful not to be obvious, Marc watched the man whenever he could. From reading history, he knew that military men who knew their enemy well waged successful campaigns.

No matter what his business at the lab, Yao found time each visit to talk with Lei. Maybe she had something to do with Marc's unscheduled trip to this unknown destination. By her own admission, she had known him in the States, after all. And Yao clearly favored her.

At lunch, Marc took a chair across from Lei. "Tease me. Tell me what you miss about the United States."

She started to speak, then stopped.

"Come on," he said. "Don't be shy."

Her tone sounded thoughtful. "Donuts."

"I miss Mexican food," he listed.

"The malls where everything is in one shopping place."

"Blockbuster movies."

She nodded. "And endless selections of music."

"Chewing gum," he added.

"Indiana University beating Purdue."

"And then," he smiled, "Purdue beating the socks off Indiana University."

"Cornhole."

"Playing basketball in the driveway with my…" His voice choked.

"Your girlfriend?"

He swallowed back the lump that lodged in his throat. "My sister."

She looked shy. "I most miss a boy I met in school."

"A fellow science major?"

She slowly spun a ring on her left hand. "A music major. Music and science have much in common."

"Especially math." Marc nodded at the gold band. "Is that from him?"

"We were engaged."

"Were?"

She shrugged. "Maybe we still are. While at college, I received a message that my father was ill, so I came home."

"And your father?"

"He's dead."

"But—"

She quickly stood. "He was dead when I returned."

Watching her leave, her lunch forgotten, Marc felt like he'd drastically overstepped. Not that he counted himself fluent in foreign common courtesy. And this place seemed to have rules of its own. What does a captive say to a fellow lab worker? How's the weather? What's your view on the latest movie? Read any good research lately? Do you know a quick way out of here?

Chapter Seventy-two

In record time, a laboratory was established and equipped in a bulky hangar on the largest Air Base in the Midwest. Several top electrical and flight engineers, known for their innovative contributions to modern propulsion, were assigned to the new project.

Mr. Spencer reported as much to his dinner partner. "The United States military is building the device from the patent."

Colonel Yao sat across from the distasteful man at a gentlemen's club in London. Great Britain had been chosen as the neutral meeting place. Flights into Heathrow were frequent and easy to procure. A major crossroads for travelers from all over the world, the airport personnel were accustomed to seeing and serving a rainbow of people of varied cultures and ethnic backgrounds. A mere six-hour flight for each of them, the two men from opposite sides of the globe could meet and return to their duties after a brief absence.

Yao had come at the insistence of the mercenary. Mr. Spencer had new information he wouldn't send by any method that could be tracked and traced. They must meet in person. "What makes you think the facility is for that exact design?"

Dressed in European slacks and cuffed shirt, Spencer had draped his herringbone jacket over the back of his chair. Yao noted that the spy flaunted expensive clothes anytime his wardrobe did not interfere with his usual need to stay invisible. This occasional indulgence flattered his ego and served as a buffer between who he had been as a homeless orphan in a third world country and where he frequented now. Through his own investigations, Yao knew this much about the mercenary.

"I studied the supplies, and they match."

A waitress served a scotch on the rocks in a squat glass to Mr. Spencer and placed a rum and coke on a napkin in front of the Colonel.

"I'm not worried." The Chinese man leisurely took note of the other patrons around them. He had exchanged the uniform of his country for the double-breasted suit of an international businessman. Though his dinner companion caused him to be tense, Yao schooled himself to appear relaxed in the rich surroundings of heavy, dark furniture under polished chandeliers. Oversized paintings depicted red-jacketed riders on white steeds galloping through thick forests beside baying dogs in pursuit of a skittish fox. The collection of large rooms smelled of furniture polish, men's cologne, expensive alcohol, and more expensive cigars. "We have the advantage of time. We began work on the project before their government passed the idea through the bureaucracy. Fools, they didn't even know what they had."

Spencer took a long drink of his scotch. Swirling the clear liquid in the glass, he smacked his full lips. "Don't underestimate them."

The Colonel lowered his voice. "Are you underestimating me?"

"Merely warning you not to get too impressed with your own press."

A short-skirted woman who circulated among the customers came to them and offered several different brands of costly cigars. Yao selected one and peeled the cellophane wrapper. "Remember that I have the inventor."

Spencer chose a cigar and let his fingers linger against the woman's hand. Suggestively, Spencer held the cigar to his nose and inhaled slowly. "Rolled on the thighs of brown skinned women."

The Colonel ignored the comment and waved away the woman.

"How long have you had him?" Spencer lit his cigar. "How much progress have you made?"

Yao frowned and blew smoke at his companion. "If it takes us a while to get the device working with the inventor, it will take the competition longer without him."

"If that logic helps you sleep at night, but I've seen surprising events when these brains get together." He signaled to the waiter for a refill of his scotch. "What incentive does your inventor have to complete the project?"

The question was the same one Yao had been asking himself. Seeing the crafty Mr. Spencer study his face, Yao once more masked his emotions behind a placid expression. Spencer's eyes narrowed. He sat back and crossed his legs, an oily smile on his face. Spencer knew he had touched his employer's soft white underbelly, and Yao suspected this to be the opportunity he anticipated. Spencer had orchestrated the setup for the little man to unveil what he really wanted from this appointment.

"Perhaps your man needs a refresher. A reminder of what his lack of cooperation will cost his sister."

The Colonel thoughtfully spun his glass in a slow circle. "You have the girl?"

"Too messy." He nodded his thanks to the waitress who efficiently removed the empty glass and, ice clinking, set a fresh drink before him. "I have an actress who looks like her and enjoys performing masochistic roles. You saw the actress on the computer screen. If you need another performance to motivate your inventor"—he smiled at the thought—"she makes situations appear real because it is."

Again, the Colonel considered this unpleasant man. A

necessary evil. Skilled at his job, he returned the required results while insulating the Colonel from contact with the virulent side of business.

"You are in a race," Mr. Spencer pressed. "If they get the device operational before you do, all of your efforts are for nothing. And I would not want to consider how your superiors will view your failure."

The Colonel gulped his drink. This man had no concept of social station. In a futile attempt to elevate himself over his employee, he issued an order. "Your job is to keep an eye on developments."

"Precisely why I insisted on this business meeting. As a show of good faith, I have the supply list from the Wright-Patterson facility. This assures that I correctly ascertained the function of the place. You need to know what your competition is doing, and I can supply you with that information." He took a long pull on the cigar. "Now let's talk financial terms."

Chapter Seventy-three

Colonel Yao had made his rounds again this morning. He bent close to Lei, and Marc watched her discreetly move to put distance between herself and the older man. Looking like a slow version of the Texas two-step, the Colonel eased his way close, and she politely found an excuse to put space between them. At last, she found a plausible reason to move to another part of the lab.

After the Colonel left, Marc made his way to Lei's workstation. She sat with her head in her hands.

"You okay?"

She sighed and turned her attention back to her work.

"Need a break?"

She opened her mouth to say something, then closed her lips and simply nodded. He led the way to the lunch area and served them both tea. Absently, Marc wondered if he would like tea when he got back to the United States or if the aroma would remind him of too many sour memories as a captive. *If* he got back to America. The deep longing twisted his gut.

Sitting across from him, Lei's shoulders were hunched, and she spun the ring on her left hand.

"Was your father opposed to your engagement?"

Self-conscience, she dropped her hands to her lap.

"You don't have to talk about it if you don't want," he said gently.

Lei stayed quiet as they both drank their tea.

"My father visited me at college," she said at last. "My fiancé paid for him to travel so they could meet."

"And?"

"The two men were respectful of one another. A good meeting. My father felt honored that he asked permission."

"He asked permission to marry you."

She swallowed. "Soon after my father returned home, I was summoned back because he was ill."

"But you were too late."

Her eyes filled with tears.

"I'm sorry. I know you miss him." Attempting to form a bridge, he added. "I miss my father, too."

She looked up questioningly.

"My mother and father are both dead."

She brushed away the tears before they could fall. "I found a letter in my father's effects, hidden where he knew I would find it."

"What did he say?"

"He encouraged me to follow my heart, and if my affections were with the American student, he gave his blessing." She reached for the ring once more and began to spin the band on her finger. "The letter had been dated prior to his illness. It was a copy, something he often did with special letters—keeping one for himself."

"I don't understand."

"His original letter he sent to me never arrived in the United States."

"Censored?"

Bitterness tinted her words. "For the good of the Republic."

"Then you'll return to marry soon?" Marc felt his heart race.

Dropping her eyes, she sat silent for a time. "My passport and student visa have been revoked."

"By who?" Just as quickly, his hopes plummeted into his

shoes. "Why?"

"The government says they need my skills here."

"Yeah." Her dad probably served as the only tie her government had to ensure the college student's allegiance, Marc calculated. When Lei's father died, apparently unexpectedly, someone was less than honest with the information forwarded to the United States university in a deliberate strategy to lure her back home and lock the door so she wouldn't leave again. Did the authorities know about her plans to marry an American? Would those plans matter?

"Have you had contact with your fiancé? Could he come to you?" Marc grasped for an opportunity in this situation.

"I wrote to him, but who knows if he received my letters."

"Phone?"

She shook her head. "The number, they say, is no longer in service."

That smelled fishy. "Email?"

"Returned as undeliverable."

Marc wondered if Lei's intended had merely relocated or if Lei's communications were being blocked. Apparently, Lei lived nearly captive in this place almost as much as he did. Almost. The difference appeared when she went home to a real home when not working at the lab. She had mobility outside these walls. He lived locked in that uninspiring cell.

She met his eyes. "He has graduated by now. I don't know where he is."

Chapter Seventy-four

Mallory bit the inside of her lip as she waited outside the Indiana University classroom. As Deverell had predicted, accustomed to fuel-powered designs, the Wright-Patterson engineers had hit a snag with Marc's patent.

She knew there existed a significant aspect that Marc had not worked out. He had told her that much about the design when they had steaks for lunch the day before he disappeared. But the lab crew had another goal. Their assignment focused on creating the appearance that the Meissner Device Generator was functional but flawed.

Just like she had 30 seconds ago and 20 seconds before that, Mallory checked her cell phone for messages. Mentally, she reviewed the list of leads she had already followed to a dead end in her anxious search for her brother.

The classroom door flew open, and students poured into the hall. Exchanging snarky witticisms and setting study dates, the young men and women went on to the rest of their day. Remorse ripped through Mallory's gut. Wading through syllabi and required class work, the students were training for their careers. The work was tough, but the future looked promising. She longed to be back in the innocence of academia where the hardest decisions were around establishing a schedule that balanced studies, work, and social time. For them, the world appeared full of potential. For her, the world had shriveled into a frightening black hole where bad decisions exacted their toll in dire consequences to herself, and more importantly, on those she loved. Where ruthless minds mercilessly stole whatever they wanted, and Mallory despaired of outsmarting them.

Inside the lecture hall, poster-sized pictures of inventors wallpapered the wall. At the lectern, a bespectacled professor talked with the college student Mallory had met in Marc's office the day Marc disappeared.

She held out her hand to the professor who covered it with both of his. "Thank you for arranging this meeting."

"Certainly, my dear." He adjusted his glasses and peered at her. "You look tired. Can I take you to lunch?"

Mallory shook her head. "Thanks, but I want to talk to Mr. Hebron Heath."

"Then I will leave you to it." He collected a worn briefcase. On his way out the door, he called back. "Give my regards to your brother for me."

Mallory bit her cheek to counteract the sudden lump in her throat. The professor disappeared, and she turned to the young man.

Wearing a *Li'l Abner* t-shirt, the student waited. His eyes were big in his pale face, and he shifted his weight to one side and back to the other. "You wanted to see me?"

"Talk with you." She waved him to the first row of seats. "How much do you understand about the Meissner Effect?"

"That's like asking how much I know about gravity, air flow, or ocean currents." He shrugged. "Some."

"About Marc's—Mr. Wayne's theory for a Meissner Effect Generator?"

"His lecture was clear." He frowned, thinking. "We talked more about it after class."

"You appeared to grasp the information on his notes when I met you in Dixon."

"The concept is solid." His knee bounced. "The device would

create buoyancy in magnetic fields in the same fashion as a balloon floating in air. Like a balloon that can lift things but has no need for traditional explosive fuels."

Mallory stood and paced.

Hebron's stomach growled. "Is there anything else?"

She stopped in front of him. "I'm here to offer you a practicum. An internship. It will meet the requirements for your degree."

"With Mr. Wayne?"

"Not exactly. But with the Meissner Device."

Excitement lit his eyes like a sparkler on the Fourth of July. "When?"

"How quickly can you leave?"

Hebron rifled through his backpack and took fast inventory. "Thirty minutes. But I gotta clear with my professors."

Mallory put a hand on his shoulder and walked him to the door. "I'll take care of your professors." She checked the time on her cell phone. "Be back here in forty. Ready to go."

Chapter Seventy-five

After intensive work, they were ready for a test run of the prototype. Marc made his final adjustments. By incorporating designs from his earlier inventions, and remixing the components that led to the fire in his kitchen, he expected this to levitate for several minutes and then explode.

Previously, he had built small-scale versions, but reluctant to waste the time, Marc had convinced Colonel Yao that this device required a minimum scale to be effective. In truth, Marc didn't want to waste the time doing the work twice. Nor did he have an interest in saving these people money, time, or effort. He gambled that he could somehow get out of here sooner rather than later.

The explosion might take people with it. He had never killed anyone before, and that part initially bothered him. But as his anger grew along with his worry over Mallory, his concern for the people who held him dissipated. He planned to be far enough away from the blast that, in the ensuing chaos, he would escape.

Marc put his tools onto the wheeled cart and rolled it back. The nervous project leader eyed Marc eagerly. "Now?"

"Knock yourself out," Marc invited.

The man scurried to the pilot's seat. Others pushed back equipment and formed an expectant circle about the device. Donning protective helmet and goggles, the project leader signaled his readiness to start. Marc tensed, prepared to spring when the timing and opportunity were right.

In that moment, Colonel Yao's voice rang loud and curt with

a single command to halt. Everyone looked to the Colonel who crossed the room to stand in front of Marc.

His eyes bore into Marc's. "You will start the machine."

Marc stared back at the man who stood shorter than himself but confident in his power. The room fell quiet, all eyes were on the two locked in an unspoken challenge.

Marc weighed his options. In the pilot's seat, he could possibly pull some wires to prevent the device from starting. Or he could explode with it, taking as many of them with him as possible. But that wouldn't help him locate Mallory.

At last Marc shrugged, hoping he looked more nonchalant than he felt. "Suit yourself."

He roughly shouldered Yao aside and waved the other man out of the pilot's seat. Buckling the helmet strap under his chin, he stared at Yao and hoisted himself into the cockpit. He adjusted the goggles when, for the second time, Yao's voice halted progress.

"Come on up," Marc invited. "You can be the first to—"

With a sly smile, Yao waved to two men standing sentry at the double doors. One quickly opened the door, and a soldier escorted someone inside. Lei.

Chapter Seventy-six

The drive from the college campus to Ohio took three hours. Thankfully, Mallory began the trip by ordering grilled burgers from the drive-through. Three for Hebron plus fries, and an extra-large milkshake to her single burger and water. They finished their meals at the same time and Hebron wondered how girls could eat so slowly.

They passed fields of corn and soybeans, wheat and the occasional sunflowers, each nearing time for harvest. Hebron realized his day had quickly transformed from another day in class toward his degree to going to another state with Marc Wayne's sister.

"So, what exactly will I be doing?" Because his professor had assured him this was a rare opportunity not to be missed, Hebron had said yes before he knew much about what he said yes to.

"With your understanding of the Meissner Device concept," Mallory tossed her burger wrappings into the empty fast-food bag, "perhaps you can bridge the gap between theory and reality."

He studied her. Was she joking? "That's a lot to expect from a lowly college student."

She mumbled something about desperate times require desperate measures.

Glancing out the window, he considered the confusing habit many adults had of voicing aloud questions and comments that would be best left unspoken. "Where are we going?"

"Ohio."

"I know that part. We passed the Welcome to Ohio sign already."

"Wright-Patterson Air Base."

"Logical." He leaned his seat back and closed his eyes. When he woke, Mallory had turned off the highway. The massive Wright-Patterson Air Base loomed before them. At a checkpoint, Mallory showed identification and was waved through. A few more turns and she parked.

"C'mon, sleepyhead." She ushered him into the facility where the collegiate took in the scope and magnitude of the lab and froze.

"Let's go." Mallory walked briskly ahead. "They're waiting for you."

But Hebron didn't follow.

Mallory returned and waved a palm in front of his face. "Earth to science geek. Anybody home?"

"You are building it. The Meissner Device." Blinking, Hebron focused on her. "For real. In my lifetime."

She planted a hand on her hip. "Except for the part these brains can't get to function." She tapped his breastbone. "That's why you're here."

In Birkenstocks, and leading with his belly, a fellow came to greet them. He stuck out a hand to Hebron while twisting the end of his handlebar mustache with the other. "I'm Wilson. You're just in time. We're in the war room slinging ideas."

The young man fell into step behind his host and spoke low to Mallory. "Is that a skunk on his shirt? For real?"

Entering the war room, the scene looked like they had stepped onto the bridge of the Starship *Enterprise*. Several CAD systems were in use, their drawings displayed on a large screen. On one wall, vertical lists of equations and designs in primary-colored markers covered the wall. Chalk sketches were posted on another wall like snowflakes on a winter night. A delicious home-baked aroma caught everyone's attention and Birkenstocks held a platter aloft—the signal to begin because everyone sat up and, like Pavlov's dog, focused their attention on Wilson. Or rather, on his tray.

In moments, the dozen men and women had pulled up chairs and were eating generous slices of banana bread. Kids' toys appeared and were tossed from person to person.

"Wilson used to be an Imagineer." Mallory caught a Super Ball and pressed it into Hebron's hand. "His unconventional methods have a surprising ability to unlock untapped possibilities." She tapped a finger against her temple.

"Think fast," someone called and silly putty landed in Hebron's lap.

Molding the familiar substance, he was instantly transported back to childhood, pressing putty against the Sunday comics. Even then, his favorite strip had been *Li'l Abner*. He leaned close to talk to Mallory over the noisy room. "Imagineers are the master planners, the creative development, designers, engineers, and production all rolled in one. The research and development of the worldwide Disney kingdom is cutting edge."

"I know." There was sarcasm in her tone.

Wilson spoke around a mouthful. "The kid is here." Using his chunk of bread as a pointer, he waved Hebron to address the group.

Chapter Seventy-seven

"She will be the first." Yao waved the young woman to the machine.

Marc bent to pull wires, but strong hands grabbed his arms and jerked him free of the machine. "Wait," Marc demanded. "There are a few adjustments—"

While two soldiers held Marc's arms, his helmet was unbuckled, and the goggles pulled from the would-be pilot's head by the stern Yao. He handed both to Lei. "It is a great honor for you to pilot the maiden flight."

Catching her eye, Marc shook his head. "Don't, Lei. Don't!" He turned to Yao. "It's my machine, let me. For heaven's sake, let me. Not her."

Through narrowed eyes, Yao stared at Marc but spoke to Lei. "Start the machine."

Marc struggled to pull free as Lei climbed into the cockpit.

"You monster," Marc accused through gritted teeth.

"Who is the monster? What do you have to worry about, Mr. Wayne?" He moved to the outer circle with the others. Again, Marc struggled futilely against the two who held him.

"Whenever you are ready," Yao called to Lei.

She leaned forward to begin the startup sequence.

"Stop! Stop, Lei!" Marc craned his neck around to get Yao's attention. "Tell her to stop, for God's sake."

Yao put up his hand in a signal for Lei to wait. He came to face him, his nose almost touching Marc's. "You underestimate me. I know about your booby trap. In fact, I expected you to do something this stupid."

He snapped his fingers, and someone brought him a file. He flashed several sheets of paper in front of Marc. Recognition flooded Marc's thoughts as he stared at his original patent design. The one he had submitted to the United States Patent Office.

"You maggot." Marc spit the words. "Where did you get those?"

"The fact is that I have them. The second fact is that I know when you deviate from the design." With the unexpected fury of a coiled snake, Yao backhanded Marc. The blow stung, and Marc felt his lip split and tasted blood in his mouth. His right eye was blurry, and Marc knew it would be a shiner within the hour.

"You are out of time." The Colonel's voice was ominous. His face close to Marc's, he jammed a finger into Marc's chest. "This is your final chance. I will have the device operational quickly or you will watch your sister be brutalized and die. Just before I kill you."

Chapter Seventy-eight

Hesitantly, the college student stood. Calculating the immense brainpower in the diverse group, he couldn't think of anything intelligent to say.

"Relax." Peering at him over her glasses and looking like his grandmother, a woman in sensible shoes patted his arm. "We don't bite."

"A few of us don't even have teeth." This from a man with a crow on his chest. The younger crowd laughed.

Adjusting horn-rimmed glasses, a man in a wheelchair rapidly typed on a computer CAD system. "This is where the patent transitions from tangible to theory. The Meissner Device is buoyant in magnetic current, but the means of propulsion is not defined." Images flashed across the screen and stopped. "Like oceanic currents, like atmospheric fluxations, the magnetic fields are only partially predictable. Corona discharges and sunspots are magnetic anomalies. The sun's poles reverse every 22 years. The current—pun intended"—he snorted at his own joke—"challenge is to accurately detect and compensate for these spastic variances, so the machine floats in space."

Wilson crammed the last of his slice of bread into his mouth. "What do you have for us, kid?"

Stuffing his hands into his jeans pockets to hide their nervous shaking, Hebron addressed the brainstorming group. "In sophomore physics, we learned the exclusionary properties of a superconductor. Theoretically, we can define a device to project an exclusionary boundary that would levitate an object. This should work." He shrugged. "But no one has come up with a device that projects such an exclusionary boundary so that magnetic fields are prevented from entering it."

He cleared his throat and noted the faces of the engineers around him. To his obvious great relief, they were not laughing. Or yawning. Or ignoring him. "The Meissner effect is a misnomer in the sense that it works more like a superconductor to levitate a magnet. Mr. Wayne's theory is to loop a superconductor flow like a hula hoop, so it continues."

"No fuel. No explosives." The only attendee in a military uniform, O'Leary unwrapped a fresh cigar and stuck it between his teeth.

As Hebron focused on science, his intimidation of the group he addressed dissipated. "Earth has a magnetic field. The sun is an electromagnetic dynamo. The moon has a magnetic anomaly with a molten magnetic core. On the moon, the local magnetic anomaly is caused by the concentration of metals under the moon's surface. Magnetic fields such as these are probably only three dynamic situations that are possible." He ticked off the list on his fingers. "It's a control challenge to compensate for the changing magnetic currents. The same way a submarine must deal with flexing currents and varied properties of water that affect the boat's ability to float and navigate."

"Exactly." Wilson licked his fingers and pointed to the figures on the chalkboard. "That's where we are in the process." Wilson eyed Mallory, then Hebron. "According to our bosses, you are the one who can take this project to the next vital step."

Hebron flushed with excitement. "There is a way to manipulate magnetic poles and control them."

Chapter Seventy-nine

Blood trailed down his chin and dripped on the design for the Meissner Device. Marc wiped his sleeve across his bleeding lip.

Ugly and hopeless, despair descended. He felt as equally ineffective to disentangle his mind from the life-sucking despondency, as to devise an escape. What was happening to Mallory? Did his actions today further endanger her? Would the Colonel set him down again in front of the computer screen, give him popcorn, and say the words over the phone that allowed her to be brutalized?

Lei appeared in front of him with a first aid kit.

"Go away." His words sounded as fat as his lip. He saw a momentary hesitation in her expression, but she dug antiseptic from her box and splashed a generous amount on a sterile gauze pad. When she looked up and wiped fresh blood with the bitter medicine, she had masked her emotions.

The liquid stung, and Marc pulled away like every guy in the movies when a girl cleaned his fight wounds. She waited for him to hold still and pressed the cotton against his lip. Probably alcohol, the stuff smelled like Mallory's nail polish remover and their evenings as a family in the living room when they were kids. The living room where he had last seen his sister being hurt by Yao's beasts. The memory stung more than the antiseptic, and he shivered. The strange reaction surprised him, and he sensed his body experiencing some level of shock.

Lei noticed his response. "I'm sorry." She threw away the

bloody wipe and doused fresh gauze with the stinging liquid. He reached to do the cleaning himself.

"I'll do it." Her tone told him not to argue, and he didn't feel up to another confrontation. The last one had not gone well. Since she didn't appear to be planning to slug him or beat him with the first aid kit, he sat quietly under her ministrations.

After bloodying Marc's lip, the Colonel had left, his anger tangible through his usual silence. The tension he brought each time he entered a room had gone out with him.

Lei snapped an instant ice pack, activating the chemicals inside, and handed the cold pack to him. "Hold this over your eye."

His bruised eye closed under the cool pack, he glanced sidelong with his good eye at the others in the lab. Similar dramatic events in the States would be talked about, opined, dissected, and verbally processed by employees meeting in small groups. Mixing around the water fountain, in the restrooms, lunchrooms, and parking lots, Americans would exercise their freedom of speech. Harassment charges would be filed. If the issue proved especially theatrical, news would leak to the press. Sensational versions would air on radio, in newspapers, and on the evening news. Television and radio talk show hosts would milk as much ratings as could be squeezed by firing up the event with scandalous questions, completely biased statements, and interviews with non-experts. The American media followed a predictable pattern.

China didn't extend the same freedom to her populace. The Chinese were practiced at holding their thoughts and questions to themselves, processing occurrences quietly and individually.

"I thought I was the only one kept here." Lei spread ointment on his cut lip.

Marc studied her. Lei's ability to travel to the United States had been put on hold, but he had not fathomed the depth of her reality. What an irony. Consumed with his own plight under the control of the People's Republic and Colonel Yao, he had not suspected Lei to be in a similar predicament. Apparently, Lei had reached a similar conclusion, believing she alone to be under government discipline. Suddenly, their previous conversations took on a completely new dimension. Both had been reserved and danced around the truth of their situation. No wonder, Marc admitted. How would he or the girl know who to trust in this policed environment where people protected themselves and their families by keeping silent and ratting out their fellows.

She looked up, caught his stare, and blushed. Putting the lid on the ointment tube, her fingers fumbled the task. Lid and medicine fell. Trying to catch what she dropped, Lei upended the first aid kit that scattered around her feet.

The noise and movement caused several in the lab to look their way. Their expressions ranged from judgment to apathy. Everyone had extra work to make the Meissner Device functional. No one wanted to be the target of the Colonel's displeasure.

Marc picked up Band-Aids and individual packets of aspirin and added them to the kit Lei reassembled. Before she snapped the lid onto the first aid supplies, she gave him another ice pack. "For later. You might need it." She took the cold pack from his eye and inspected the damage. Standing on her tiptoes, Lei looked at him meaningfully. "You may need help."

Chapter Eighty

Skunk Works. Hebron was part of an esteemed Skunk Works team, and he couldn't tell anyone. This would so impress the brainiac college girls with the delicious figures. He imagined the female collegiates clustered around him while he dropped just enough of the story to keep their eyes on him, their hands caressing his neck.

"I said let's launch this puppy." The authoritative voice broke into Hebron's daydream.

Talking around the perpetual cigar when he wasn't chewing on it, Major Orson O'Leary was in charge of the group that functioned with a high degree of autonomy unhampered by bureaucracy, despite the fact that they were quartered on a military base.

In the short time he had been at the lab, Hebron had encountered men and women with patches depicting skunks and crows. They were legends. Skunks were the elite engineers. Ravens were the electronics specialists. Old Crows were retired but couldn't keep away. They often showed up for the occasional consult or project.

The official trademark for the Lockheed Martin Advanced Development Programs, Skunk Works projects were developed by a small, loosely structured group of experts who researched and developed purely for the sake of prototype innovation. The name was influenced by Al Capp's comic strip, *Li'l Abner*. Popular in the 1940s and 1950s, the hillbilly strip featured a dilapidated

factory located in backwoods Kentucky on the outskirts of
Dogpatch. From skunks and old shoes, Skonk Works brewed and
barreled skonk oil.

Similarly, the original Lockheed facility was located next to a
malodorous plastics factory. As a gag, one day an engineer showed
up at work in a gas mask. The neighboring smell, and the secrecy
of the work, inspired workers to name the facility after the comic
strip factory. When a Skunk Works team member answered a call
from the Department of the Navy with "Skonk Works," the name
stuck. In compliance with a request from the *Li'l Abner* copyright
holders, Lockheed changed the name of the advanced development
company to Skunk Works.

In 1943, in dire need of a jet to counter the superior German
models, the US Army met with Lockheed. Young and brilliant
engineer Clarence "Kelly" L. Johnson and his team delivered the
XP-80 one month later. Four months before the formal contract
arrived. The prototype team commonly delivered a requested
project on a handshake. Working under Kelly's 14 rules and
practices, projects were always delivered ahead of schedule and
without a contract or official submittal process.

Hebron suspected the absence of ridiculous paperwork freed
these geniuses to create. Wisely, Johnson had given his team the
liberty to function free from bureaucratic constraints. Today, ahead
of schedule, the team prepared to launch the Meissner Device.

Hebron wore his lucky *Li'l Abner* t-shirt. Everyone who had a
role in the project had shown up. Project team members took their
places and excited talk quieted. O'Leary pointed his cigar, and
Hebron began the sequence. Acting as a superconductor, the
machine emitted a hum as it generated energy to repel natural
magnetic currents. Lab personnel were proud of the sound created
by their work. Like parents tuned in to their infant's coos, to hear
the device's voice as the project progressed, engineers and
designers gradually turned down their personal music sources

spouting everything from Wilson's classical orchestras to Hebron's heavy metal.

Slowly, the Meissner Device lifted from its platform. The machine levitated for several minutes, and Skunks and Old Crows whooped and gave each other high-fives. With a nod from O'Leary, Hebron pushed the remote controls, and the device jerked forward. The momentum caused the invention to wobble like a Friday night drunk.

"She's gonna sun her moccasins." O'Leary wheeled his arm in a circle toward the hangar wall. "Now, Mr. Heath!"

Chapter Eighty-one

Tonight, like every previous night, Marc lay on his back, fingers laced behind his head. Staring at the high ceiling, he took mental inventory. In his mind, he had two lists. One consisted of materials available to him. Items in the lab. The second cataloged the people in this place of confinement and in order of their strengths and weaknesses. To these details, he added the fact that the Chinese were preparing to celebrate National Day.

With a ceremony at Tiananmen Square, the People's Republic of China had been founded on October 1, 1949. Through nationally organized festivities, people celebrated the annual holiday. Representing the People's Republic of China, and to keep the populace from getting frisky, the military would make a showing. No doubt, Colonel Yao would attend perfunctory events. Like Fourth of July in the United States, cities decorated in patriotic themes, and orchestras performed extravagant concerts followed by bright fireworks.

Fireworks. He bolted up and sat on the edge of the bed as segments of ideas rapidly connected. Pacing now, Marc outlined a plan. Hours later, feeling at last he had a direction worth pursuing, he collapsed back onto the cot. But sleep eluded him. Instead, he felt something he'd not possessed since his abduction. Lightheartedness driven by possibility. Adrenaline springing from a fresh sense of options. He felt hope.

Chapter Eighty-two

In the small garden at his house, Colonel Yao paced. The offensive Mr. Spencer had been right. The Americans were developing their own Meissner Device. Had apparently even got the thing airborne. No matter that the vehicle had crashed. Much like the previous race to the moon, the engineers would learn from the process, adjust the necessary figures, and launch again.

Spencer had provided additional information that a solution to the misfire had been found in the office of the patent's author. Marc Wayne knew how to make the device work. As Yao had suspected, the American was stalling.

Hearing a sound, he turned to see his housekeeper bring an envelope. A single letter. Like clockwork.

Sitting on a garden bench he realized he had scanned the length of the correspondence with his eyes and not paid attention to what the words said. His current worries dominated his thoughts. The development of the Meissner machine must be completed in China first.

The housekeeper returned with a tray. Silently, she poured tea and left again. Sipping the infusion of flowers and leaves, he harnessed his galloping thoughts and began to read the letter again.

The news in the village was typical. A marriage, two babies, and the condition of the rice fields now that they had water systems. "Our only wish, my son, is for a grandson before we die."

Chapter Eighty-three

In the lab the next day, Marc bent close to Lei at her workstation. "I have an idea."

She kept solemnly focused on her work, poised to listen.

"It will be dangerous. If you don't want to be involved, just do something."

She froze.

He shook his head. "Okay, not too effective. Look, if you'd rather not be involved, scratch your nose."

Instead, she inclined her head to hear more.

Now Marc froze. If she accompanied him, he felt he had a better shot with a partner. She knew this country, customs, and language. Her deep longing to be reunited with the man she loved, the one she planned to spend the rest of her life with, counted as a heady motivation. But if she came with him, could he guarantee her safety?

Lei dropped a spool of wire. The spool bounced and rolled before she retrieved and set the object in front of him. "What?"

He picked up wire cutters, stripped plastic from a length and spliced bare wires onto a connector. "I think that while the big shots are away for the celebration, we can pull it off."

A lab worker stepped over. "What are you doing?"

Marc glanced up absently at the intrusion. "Working. Same as you." Marc kept eye contact until the intruder looked away and returned to his work area. *It was all a game of chicken. Who would flinch first?*

With exaggerated motions for anyone who watched, Marc pulled a pencil from behind his ear and reached for paper. He scribbled formulas along the margins as he wandered to a desk. Some time later, Colonel Yao leaned over his shoulder.

"Tell me about your work."

Marc didn't bother to look up. He didn't want his eyes to betray him. "I have some new ideas I want to try out." *That was certainly true.*

"Good."

"Allow me access to the laboratory over the next couple days. I believe I can make a breakthrough in the controls to divert and intensify the output field."

Colonel Yao moved beside him and clasped his hands behind his back. He stood quiet for several moments. When he didn't get a response, Marc stood and faced the man.

"What are you afraid of? That I'll escape?" Frustrated, he gestured to include the large sanctuary that had been transformed from a place of spiritual worship to a gathering that paid homage to technology. "From this fortress? Don't you think I've already considered every possible means of getting out of here?"

The Colonel stared at him.

"Look," Marc reasoned, sounding desperate. "I know the only chance I have of going home is to get this machine to fly. I'd like to be home by Christmas."

The Colonel remained cool. Weighing. Calculating.

Marc flopped back into his seat, his back to the cold Colonel. "Forget it."

The man remained behind Marc. Yao's presence made the hair stand up on the back of Marc's neck. *Creepy.* After a silence so long that Marc truly grew desperate, the Colonel spoke.

"Very well. You work during celebration."

Chapter Eighty-four

At an all-night diner in Dayton, Ohio, Mr. Spencer drank coffee as dark as the night outside. Beside his cup sat a thermos. He checked the time on his cell phone. Thumbing to his email account, he reread the report. Satellites had detected a change in the facility he watched at Wright-Patterson for Colonel Yao.

Outside the greasy spoon's side windows, a set of headlights marked the arrival of a small pickup that had been used hard. Wearing scuffed work boots and a dark blue janitorial uniform, a lanky man emerged.

Moments later, the man sat across from Spencer in the restaurant booth.

"You're late."

With a hand calloused and dry with age, the man pulled a stocking cap from his graying head. "Takes longer to do my job."

"How long does it take to round up and destroy trash?"

He ran knuckly fingers over his close-cropped hair. "That hangar with the new activity is the trouble."

A thick-waisted waitress brought a second cup. At Spencer's signal, she left the coffee pot on their table.

"It's off-limits, so gotta use lengthier procedures. Thar's a hole in the side of the hangar. A big hole. Rumor is that it was a forklift accident." He shook his head. "No way. I drive a forklift. Nothin' to it after the first time. No, sir. That damage is too large and too high for a forklift."

Spencer draped an arm across the back of the booth. "What

does it look like to you?"

"Sounds crazy, but looks like something flew through the metal wall." He picked at something between his teeth. "All this goin's on. Somethin' in there and you keepin' my baby-gal in college for havin' coffee with you regular. Keepin' that thermos supplied with papers I find." He whistled softly between his teeth.

Spencer twisted the lid from the thermos, filled it with coffee from the pot, and slid it to his companion.

The man exchanged the now full thermos for the look-alike he had carried in from the truck. "Thanks for the coffee." He tugged on his sock hat and disappeared into early morning darkness in the rattling pickup.

Chapter Eighty-five

Mallory turned into Thomas's driveway and parked. He had invited her to dinner and to meet the new baby.

Since her brother disappeared, she felt consumed with guilt. Passing homes with families gathered for dinner increased her regret. "I was only thinking of myself," she said aloud. "I sacrificed Marc to the wolves." Knowing she would not be good company, she leaned her forehead against the steering wheel. "It's my fault. My stupid choices."

A knock on the driver's window made her look up. Thomas peered at her. She waved him away, but he stubbornly stood there. Waiting. In the evening light, she could see concern in his eyes. She didn't deserve his empathy or compassion. She didn't deserve anything.

Thomas pointed to the lock on the door. Instead, she rolled down the window halfway.

"Are you okay?"

Her jaw tight against embarrassing emotions, Mallory nodded.

"Come on in."

She shook her head. "Not a good idea. Tell your family I'm sorry, but I can't do this."

Thomas reached through the window and unlocked the car doors. He walked around the front of her car and seated himself on the passenger side. He spoke gently. "Talk to me."

"I can't."

"Why not?"

"If I start, I will cry."

He shifted in the seat to face her. "Mallory, you gotta talk. This is more than the case, isn't it?"

She pulled a loose sting from the bottom of her sweater and wound it around her finger, unwound it, and wound it again.

"Okay. What else?"

"I sent my brother into the hands of our enemies. Maybe to his death. What kind of murderer am I? I put work ahead of my family. Ahead of the person who means the most to me."

"What else?"

She bit back the humiliating self-talk that had beat in her brain like a tribal drum. *You sent your brother to his death.* She shook her head to his question.

"What, Mallory? What is it?" His voice sounded tender, the way she imagined he spoke with his children. The way her dad, the way Marc would probe her hurt feelings.

She took a chance. Vulnerable and raw, the words exploded out. "I'm an atrocious failure." Angrily, she pressed knuckles to her stinging eyes to stop tears that she refused to allow. "A failure as a research analyst, a failure as a daughter. A failure as a sister."

She waited for him to contradict her.

"I'm certain you feel that way." He fished in the glove box and pulled out a handful of fast-food napkins. "It looks pretty dark right now."

"What if we never find him? Never know what happened to my brother?"

"We'll find him. I know we will."

"So much time has passed. Is he hurt? Maimed? Or psychologically damaged beyond repair?"

"Mal, you can't torture yourself like this. It clouds your ability to do your job. To follow the leads to find him."

"I had a thousand options, and I chose to exploit my brother.

The sacrificial lamb to bait the thieves. I thought only of myself. Of the easiest ways to make my idea, my plan, work. To solve the case quickly and," she did her best imitation of Deverell, "get some good PR." She landed a fist on the armrest. "Recognition and a promotion. Accolades."

The front door of the house opened. A blanketed bundle in her arms and silhouetted in the yellow light streaming from the living room, a tall woman peered out. Thomas gazed at his wife. "You didn't make the decision in a vacuum. I agreed. So did Deverell."

"This is all because of my choice. I chose to put Marc in danger."

Two young children pushed in front of each other, tumbling onto the front porch like puppies. "How is beating yourself up helping you find Marc?"

Thomas waved the international okay sign to his family. His wife nodded and, with a word, rounded up the children and pointed them inside. She gave a wave to Mallory and Thomas in the car and disappeared inside, closing the front door behind her.

Mallory stared unseeing out the windshield. "If Mom and Dad were alive, they would be so disappointed that I jeopardized Marc. Disappointed in me."

Thomas stretched his arm across the back of their seats. He touched her shoulder. "It's pretty hard to fight a ghost, Mallory. Let your parents rest in peace."

Noisily, she blew her nose. "I pray that Marc isn't a ghost."

"It's not over till it's over. Keep the faith. Give the process a chance."

"If we do find him—"

"*When* we find him."

"How will I face him?" She swallowed against the choking lump in her throat. "Look what I've done to our relationship. The two of us are all we have. And I betrayed him."

"I have a large family, and I would feel the same way if any one of them were harmed. I know how important Marc is to you."

"Mom and Dad were giddy when they brought him home. An infant," she waved a hand toward the house, "like your new baby."

Thomas reached for the door. "Let my wife feed you a good home cooked meal."

She went back to winding the string around her finger. "Marc brought a heightened sense of life and purpose to our family."

He eyed her. "Who knows when you last ate something healthy."

"Marc completes us. My parents adored him."

"Come on in, Mallory." Thomas got out of the car. "Play with the kids and hold the baby. It'll be good medicine."

She nodded.

As soon as the passenger door closed, Mallory put the car in reverse. In her rearview mirror, she saw Thomas standing in the driveway, watching her drive away.

Chapter Eighty-six

Marc looked up as Colonel Yao approached the table where he and Lei ate. Disregarding Marc, Yao spoke to Lei in Chinese.

Ignoring the snub, Marc took advantage of the situation to study his nemesis. He noticed something on Yao's hand he had not noticed before. In fact, he felt sure the jewelry had not been there previously. Why now?

So, the Colonel graduated from the East Coast's illustrious university for geniuses. MIT's class ring, often called the Brass Rat, is uniquely crafted each year. Though the mascot looks like a rat, the beaver was selected as the engineer of the animal world. Marc knew that in the world, there are three recognizable rings: the West Point ring, the Super Bowl ring, and the MIT Brass Rat. As Marc had suspected, the Colonel wanted to impress the lovely, young Lei. This information had to be useful. Somehow.

Turning his attention back to the conversation, Marc watched surprise cross Lei's face. The Colonel waited. Lei appeared to consider her answer before looking back at the waiting Yao. She demurred for a moment. Then her eyes met Marc's. He noted a flash of inspiration, but the look disappeared so quickly, he wondered if he had imagined what he saw.

She turned a flattered expression to the brooding Colonel. With a gentle smile, she nodded. Looking cautiously pleased, he gave a slight bow and left.

Marc watched her push her food around on her plate. "You okay?"

She met his gaze. "He invited me to accompany him to the formal festivities on National Day."

Chapter Eighty-seven

In a vehicle across the street from a strip mall, Mallory watched several moms with babies in strollers.

Four moms and three strollers. The fourth mother held a preschooler by the hand. In her other hand she carried a protest sign. *Jesus loves the little children.* The reverse side read, *It's a child, not a choice.*

On a Thursday morning, the mothers patrolled the front of a family planning clinic. A car parked, and a mother intercepted the young girl before she entered the building. During a brief conversation between the women, accompanied by tears, the preschooler pressed into the girl's hand a palm-sized baby doll, a replica of a baby at eight-weeks' gestation.

From the passenger side of the car, an unkept young man got out. Wresting the sign from the mother's hand, he snapped it in half and threw the pieces. Snatching the pamphlet from the girl, he waved the flier in her face. She cowered while he shredded the paper to tiny pieces that scattered around their feet like snowflakes. Over the loud objections of the protesting mother, he twisted the girl's arm behind her back, pried the small doll from her hand, and ground the small form underfoot on the gritty asphalt.

A nurse came from the clinic, elbowed the women away, and escorted the girl inside. With a final glare, the man returned to wait in the car.

The drama saddened Mallory. Somewhere she had read that there were many adoptive parents whose arms remained empty while abortion numbers climbed. Aware that abortion was an option, her parents had prayed daily that Marc's biological mom would carry him to term. She shuddered to consider how close Marc might have come to having his life ended in a place like the one the girl had entered. Wondering what meat grinder held him now made her want to vomit.

But she waited for a different person to arrive. Someone that might have information about her brother. After talking with the pilot of the medical flight, she had followed a sketchy trail to find the doctor who had been aboard the plane with Marc. Finding him resembled chasing a grasshopper. His spastic schedule mirrored the erratic jobs he did. Mallory had to be certain she had located the right guy. And that he would be at this location.

An hour later, her early morning vigil yielded her answer when a black limo pulled to the clinic's back door. The suited driver trotted to the passenger side and swung open the door. Dressed in Dockers and a polo shirt, a long-legged man stepped out. He tipped back the last of a cocktail and handed the empty glass to the driver.

Mallory glanced at the time. She considered the hour early in the day to be getting hammered but perhaps that helped him execute what he did in this place. A dozen cars, including the one with the surly man, had delivered young ladies to the address. A middle-aged woman who checked her watch and drove away brought three teenage girls. Mallory suspected her to be the campus nurse from the local high school.

Pushing their strollers, the mothers crossed the street and got into their minivans near where Mallory watched. Cradling her sleeping child, the preschooler's mother tapped on Mallory's passenger window. Mallory beckoned her inside.

"Did you see him?"

Mallory nodded.

"The clinic is not licensed to perform abortions. We pressured the health department for an inspection but that proved useless. The inspector warned them when he planned to arrive and ignored the obvious." In her arms, she adjusted the child that snored slightly. "Killing babies is lucrative."

"Why not just use a local doc?"

The mother tilted her head. "We let the word out that some folks' trusted family physicians were cutting little babies to pieces. It was embarrassing and not good for business."

They watched the angry young man get out of the car once again and walk aimlessly. "You demonstrated in front of the doctor's house?"

The youngster passed gas, and the mother wrinkled her nose and patted the small bottom. "The strategy worked for a while. The abortions stopped. Then the clinic brought in this guy from out of the area." She rolled down the window and waved goodbye to the other women as they drove away.

Across the street, the young man who had chosen not to be a father, lit a cigarette

.

"Thank you for your help," Mallory said to her companion.

"Hope the information I gave you will help us stop this." She opened the car door and carefully got out without disturbing her daughter's sleep. "The children who are dying in there are contemporaries of my children. The would-be neighbors, friends, and maybe the spouse of my girl." She glared toward the clinic. "The Constitution says everyone—e v e r y o n e—has the right to life. Even preborn babies. The Bible says, 'thou shall not kill.' Those fiends belong in jail with the rest of the criminals and murderers." She planted a kiss on the still sleeping child's forehead and left.

Across the street, the young man lit another cigarette and disappeared into the convenience store next door. Through the window, Mallory watched him purchase a soda and drop coins into the video game machine.

Hunched over, the girl Mallory had seen escorted into the clinic, shuffled stiffly out. No one escorted her on the return trip to her car. Even her cantankerous companion didn't wait there for her. Looking fraught, she searched her surroundings and finally made her way to the convenience store. Playing another game, the young man didn't look up when she entered. He shrugged off the hand she put on his arm. Pleading, she began to cry. Until the video game ended, he ignored her. Then, taking the wilting girl by the arm, he propelled her outside and to their car. Lighting a cigarette, he threw the keys in her direction and got into the passenger seat. As the couple drove off, Mallory prayed the girl would disentangle herself from an obviously toxic relationship.

Using her cell phone, Mallory made arrangements for the visiting doctor's afternoon. The FBI had some questions for him. Someone else would do the asking for her. Others who knew the fine arts of inquiring and obtaining advantageous information from slippery men like him.

For herself, Mallory felt eager to hear what the doctor's upcoming and unexpected appointment would reveal to her about Marc's whereabouts.

Chapter Eighty-eight

"Smoke and mirrors," Marc explained.

Day after day, night after night, Marc worried about Mallory. Where was she? What were those beasts doing to her? His imaginings were a curse, preventing him from thinking clearly. From developing a plausible plan to escape.

Once away from this prison, he needed to find his sister. When she didn't show up at work, had the FBI been searching? Had the FBI connected the fact that Marc and Mallory were both missing?

Would the Colonel's goons keep Mallory near his house where he had last seen her on Yao's computer screen? When Marc escaped, Yao would doubtless make good his threat and kill Mallory before he reached her. For his sister's best chance, Yao must be made to believe Marc died rather than escaped. He hoped to buy time to locate his sister.

The gravity of their circumstance paralyzed him from formulating a plan when he most needed to. Other times, the danger served as a fiery motivation. All the time, his thoughts bounced from escape to proving progress on the Meissner Device to keep Yao from further harming Mallory until he could find her. Marc's usually methodical thoughts now rebounded like hail on a tin roof.

Lei looked confused, and he knew he sounded as disconnected as he felt. In truth, Marc had decided to move forward with even a crackpot plan before he lost more precious time attempting to corral renegade ideas. He would take each next step that presented itself. When no plan appeared, he would figure out what to do. He no longer believed a safe, guaranteed, workable plan existed.

"We make it look like the Meissner Effect Generator works. Like we solved the problem and used the device to escape."

In her eyes he saw a guarded flicker of hope. "But where will we go?"

Marc sighed. "That's where it gets tricky. We hide."

"Hide where?"

"In plain sight. Sort of. Here in the building. They'll think we're long gone."

"But we're still stuck here."

"They will have the city locked down, and we have no idea where to go." Mark ran a hand through his hair. "I'm gambling that if they think we're gone, these goons will ease up on the security precautions around here."

"And we'll slip out."

"Right."

She frowned. "And go where?"

"That's the other tricky part."

She looked at him quizzically.

He shrugged. "Okay, it's a half-baked idea. But that's all I have."

Chapter Eighty-nine

He'd be thrown inside before anyone noticed the loss. Escorted to his cell, Marc breathed deep and gathered his courage.

When the door opened, Marc flew at the guard. He chose the largest of the two in hopes that surprise would level the fighting field. Besides, Marc knew the big fella as the first guard Marc met when he awakened in his cell, the short-fused soldier who had wanted to tear Marc's face from his head as a gift from the welcome wagon. Marc saw the intent in the man's dark eyes, and ever since, Marc had wanted to slug him.

Head down, he charged the uniformed man, bowled into his solid middle, and the two slammed to the floor. Marc threw a fist into the man's chest and another into his face before the smaller guard grabbed Marc, pulled him up, and pinned his arms. Back on his feet, the bigger guard approached Marc with narrowed eyes. The brute had wanted to punch Marc since he first saw him. Marc could see from the glint in his expression that he had every intention of enjoying this opportunity that had so easily presented itself. He slammed a fist into Marc's face.

The blow snapped back his head. Pain exploded in his brain. Strong arms tossed Marc onto the floor of his cell, and the door locked behind him.

Now for the tricky part. Face down on the floor, his hands trapped beneath him, he slyly moved his fingers. He felt what he hoped to find. He'd pulled off the deed. The guards thought he tried to make a run for it, but Marc had something else in mind.

Cautiously, he slipped the guard's stolen badge into his clothes and away from the view of the video camera monitoring his room.

Rolling to his back, he touched his face. He considered the prize worth a broken nose.

The following day, Marc's face looked like a war zone. Throbbing under the extra ice pack Lei had given him the last time he earned a black eye, his swollen nose appeared twice the normal size, and made him sound like he had a severe cold. Blood crusted inside both nostrils. He imagined he looked like something out of a horror movie his mom wouldn't let him watch as a kid. Lei gave him a concerned look. He winked back and instantly regretted the cavalier move. His face hurt like crazy.

Working through lunch, Marc had a brief time of relative privacy. He'd thought this through to require as little time as possible to execute. The core of Hebron's invention held a three-dimensional optical scanner that allowed Marc to read and duplicate the icon on the guard's badge he had pinched.

Using Hebron's diamond device, he separated the fine layers of the identification part of the badge. Then he reproduced them on a new background. The result wasn't a carbon copy of the original, but that wasn't the goal. The important part he wanted to duplicate got doors open around here. Hebron's brainchild did have more than the single function his father had rejected.

Later, he slipped his creation to Lei. "Use this to see what's in the other restricted areas. Maybe our way out."

As he walked away, she made a slight movement to adjust her bra, and Marc knew she had hidden the faux badge.

Chapter Ninety

That afternoon, the doctor left the family planning clinic
through the back door and climbed into the waiting limo. Full
metal garage music drowned out the sounds of the day as he
poured himself a snifter of brandy. The velvet liquid warmed his
throat, and he commended himself for another lucrative use of his
skills.

After his second drink, the limo parked. The driver opened
the door, and the doctor stretched his legs and stepped out.

"What the—?" He faced the same back door he'd exited two
drinks earlier. "You stupid—" He turned to curse at the inept limo
driver, but stopped when he saw the Glock pointed at his head.
Two men, one bald and the other over-muscled, appeared
seemingly from nowhere, grabbed his arms and roughly propelled
him inside.

"What's this about?" The doctor glanced at his watch. "If you
are health inspectors, you have the wrong guy. You need to track
down the director of this facility. And do it quickly. I have a plane
to catch."

"Shut up." The limo driver locked the clinic door behind
them.

The employees that had populated the clinic were gone for
the night, and the lights were off. Down the narrow hall padded
with dated rust-colored carpet, the three expressionless men
pushed the doctor. They entered a windowless back room, and the
bald man closed and blocked the door. The limo driver turned on a

single light against the evening shadows.

Smelling of mold and alcohol, the exam room had been adapted for inpatient surgery. The doctor knew this room. He had spent all day performing the same procedure over and over in this dreary place.

The man with the gun waved the weapon in his direction. The doctor sighed and half-heartedly raised his arms. The limo driver patted him down and examined his license and credit cards. He took particular interest in the large amount of big bills overflowing the alligator skin wallet.

"Look boys." The driver waved a wad of hundreds. "Killing babies pays better than what we make for killing guys like him."

"Dang. And babies don't fight back." Shorter than the other two, the guy whose face looked like he made side money in a boxing ring, ran a hand over the powerful suction machine used to pull infants from the security of their mother's womb. "Quiet even when you suck out their eyes." The boxer turned on the suction machine. "Here's lookin' at you, babe."

"Gentlemen, what do you want?" The doctor looked at his watch once more. "I'm sure we can come to a mutually satisfactory agreement."

The man with the suction machine pointed the nozzle in the direction of the doctor. "We know what this does to babies, I wonder what it can do to the doctor who uses it."

Moving toward the well-guarded door, the doctor put out his hands, palms up. "Okay, is this about a girlfriend? A daughter? Look, I don't know who they are, I just—"

"You just help them out like a good Boy Scout." The boxer dangled a latex glove in front of the nozzle. Like a beast devouring prey, the sound of the machine revved, and the glove quickly disappeared, sucked from his hand. "You're just the good doctor doin' everyone a favor."

"Just a law-abidin' citizen." The limo driver shoved the

Glock up the doctor's nostril. "What other services do you perform?"

The doctor started to shake his head but winced when the gun held his face in place. "There isn't—"

The driver twisted the gun further into his nose. "Ever been the doctor for a medical flight?"

The pain in his nose made his eyes water. "I don't know what you're talking about."

With a deep growl, the man with the misshapen nose lunged at him. Before he could back-pedal, the doctor found himself thrown onto the exam table with enough force to knock the air from his lungs. Tissue paper crackling and tearing, the doctor struggled against the attack. In seconds, the bald man and the limo driver had him strapped to the narrow medical table like a bug on a fifth-grade insect display.

The boxer brought the suction tube to hover near the doctor's face and bent close. "You won't be doing any medical procedures, legal or otherwise, if you're blind."

An electric jolt of primal fear pulsed through the doctor's veins, and he renewed his desperate attempts to free himself. Squinting to protect his eyes, he fought to turn his face away but could not. The focused black hole of the suction tube, the same one he had wielded all day, loomed near. Above the noise of the machine, he heard the boxer.

"Here's lookin' at you, babe."

Chapter Ninety-one

As he anticipated, Marc and his room were given a nasty shakedown that evening. Not that the searchers had much to look through.

Escorted to his room, Marc observed the two guards from the previous evening's brawl turning over the thin mattress, the bed frame, the table and chair, and looking for hiding places between the walls and the floor.

"You fellas lost something?" Marc couldn't resist the jab. What were they gonna do? Beat him up some more? Eventually Yao would notice, and Marc could bet they would not want to tell the Colonel they misplaced an identification badge. One of their identity classifications that got people through locked doors in this gloomy place.

Nor did Marc want them to find the incriminating ID on him after his successful heist the night before. That would trash his whole half-baked escape plan. The more time that passed, the more he felt panicked for Mallory. Earlier, Marc had slipped the badge into the women's restroom. Found there, the badge would create some interesting questions for the uniformed group and hopefully divert suspicion from him.

The big guard's eyes narrowed, and he advanced, clearly intending to work over Marc the way he had been working over the room. His two escorts held Marc as the big guy began the pat-down when a voice called from behind.

Then Lei came beside him, her tone forceful. The big guy

blanched, and the others snickered and released their hold on Marc. Small and indignant, she pushed herself between Marc and his would-be attacker. Eyes flinty with anger, she spoke fast and not in English. She swung the badge in front of the guard's face, and the others stepped back to avoid any connection to what transpired between the man and the angry scientist. Finally, she dropped the badge on the floor, spun on her heel to quickly lock eyes with Marc before turning toward the lab.

"If I ever see you anywhere near the women's room again…" Her steps were as clipped as her words, and Marc knew the last sentence had been spoken for his benefit.

Marc whistled through his teeth and wagged a finger in the no-no gesture at the guard who looked confused and humiliated as he retrieved his badge from the floor. The others punched the big guard in the shoulder and made comments Marc did not comprehend, but he understood the razzing tone.

In a flash, the guard threw a punch into Marc's gut and tossed him into the room. The door slammed. Lying on the floor, sucking in oxygen like a beached fish, Marc considered the day had been productive.

Chapter Ninety-two

Like every previous morning, a soldier escorted Marc from his room to the large double doors of the laboratory. The sentry kept his place outside the lab, while the guard followed Marc and assumed a post inside.

To keep an eye on me.

Unpopulated today, the lab was empty except for Marc and his babysitter. Everyone else would be celebrating National Day. Even Lei had accompanied the Colonel to the activities. Now. He would seize the opportunity. He had to escape, and the deed must happen today. Progressing through his mental checklist, he worked. Preparing.

When he came to the final action points, his heart pounded, and he stopped frequently to wipe damp palms against his pant leg. Nervous, he tried to remember brave characters from spy movies as inspiration. They never seemed jittery. *What would Batman do? How would the Green Hornet or Ironman figure a way out and bring down the enemy?*

A commotion at the door caused him to lose his concentration and his balance. His supplies spilled to the floor. The guard started over to check Marc's actions. Breathless, Marc scooped the scattered pieces, hoping the man with the gun at his hip would not recognize what he saw. But Marc chided himself. What military trained personnel didn't have a basic knowledge of things that blew up? They destroyed things for a living, for Pete's sake.

Fumbling to gather the most incriminating evidence before

inquiring eyes recognized them for what they were, Marc glanced up to see the narrowing eyes of the approaching soldier.

"Hey," Lei called. Marc and the soldier looked to the open doorway where the guard posted outside stood with a satisfied grin and grubby fingers wrapped around a steaming cup. Lei held out a second cup to the guard who menacingly approached Marc.

The man hesitated, and Marc's hope sunk as he recognized the big guy whose badge Marc had pinched. The one guy who particularly didn't like Marc. The same man Lei had derided when she returned his identification badge. He turned simpering whenever she looked at him. Quickly, Marc swept the last explosive element out of sight. When the guard glanced back to Marc, Marc looked longingly at the cup in Lei's hand and inhaled deeply, hoping to turn the man's attention to the proffered coffee. He also hoped the deep breath would calm his own rising panic.

Lei shrugged and carried the cup in Marc's direction.

"Thanks," he said, and tipped the cup to his lips. His eyes on Lei, he saw her frown.

With a grunt, the guard grabbed the coffee from Marc and took a long drink. With a smirk, he waved Lei aside to her work and returned to the door where both guards downed the contents of their drinks and talked quietly.

"Once they're asleep, we have maybe two hours," she said softly.

Marc brushed sweat from his forehead. "What's in those cups?"

She cast a sidelong glance at the men. "Benadryl, I brought back from the States."

"How much?"

"A lot."

He glanced at the guards and puffed out his cheeks. "Let's get to work."

The futuristic-looking vehicle had taken shape under Marc's

direction. Now, he worked under his own plan, one outlined not on paper but solely in his mind. Lei reassembled the items that had spilled, and Marc set the explosives in strategic places.

"What about the Colonel?"

She glanced at the clock. "He is where he's supposed to be with other dignitaries. The fireworks will begin soon."

"Will he be looking for you? His date?"

"I told him I had a headache and had to go home." She handed him the mixture which he strategically pressed into place. "What happens after it explodes?"

"That's where things gets dicey. We have to squirrel into a hiding place, so the Colonel and his boys think we're gone."

He glanced across the room. The doors were closed which meant one guard kept post outside while his partner remained inside. After a yawn, the man in view tossed back the final swallow of the tainted coffee before crushing and tossing the disposable cup into the trash. "What's in the other areas of this facility?"

"There is a heavy amount of security at the far end."

"Did you use the badge? Get a look inside?"

"Briefly." She spoke softly. "It's full of weapons. And big boxes."

"Weapons." Marc thought this over.

"And boxes."

"Is there an opening for shipping?" He indicated the wall opposite the entry where the guards were posted. "Like the doors in here that open to the cargo ships?"

Her eyes went to the large doors along the waterside wall. "Yes, there are doors like that in there."

Marc continued his way around the Meissner Device, turning over Lei's information about the cordoned off hallway in hopes of figuring their next step. With everything set, he approached her. "Look, you can leave now. It would be safer for you."

She drew herself up. "I'm going with you."

"Really, Lei. No one will ask any questions or suspect you of anything." He indicated the world outside the cargo doors. "Stay here in your homeland."

"This place is no longer my home." She shook her head. "I have no reason to remain."

"Have the enviable positioned life as the young wife of the Colonel, for Pete's sake."

She lifted her chin. "Let's go."

Seeing the guard slumped in a chair, asleep by the door, Marc dropped a wrench. The tool clanged loudly to the floor, but the guard merely twitched and slept on. "This is beyond risky, Lei. We may kill ourselves or get killed."

She nodded.

"Are you sure?"

"I'm sure."

"Lei—"

Putting both hands on his shoulders, she shoved him into action. "Let's go before I realize what I just said."

Chapter Ninety-three

Arnold Taylor admired the woman in front of him. Half his age, she worked as an actress on New York's Broadway stage; that is when she wasn't entertaining him.

Taylor fancied himself as Aristotle Onassis, and she served as his Maria Callas. But he never told her of his fantasy. He would not trust this intimacy to anyone. The fragile illusion belonged only to his ability to bring imagination to reality.

He had first seen her when he brought his wife to New York. The excitement of the long-deferred trip and the show-stopping Broadway performance resulted in a migraine. At their hotel, he tucked her into bed with a cold cloth on her forehead. Then he ventured out into the night for a stroll in the Big Apple and maybe a drink.

His wife believed the visit to New York City to be an anniversary celebration, and he let her treat him like a hero. After months of suspense, the first product had been delivered to the sly man who had approached the aging Taylor with a business proposition. A secret bank account proved that this new side job paid better than his career position at the United States Patent and Trademark Office.

On his walk that first night in the big city, he happened upon a party in the hotel's upscale restaurant and bar. High on performance adrenaline, a number of the cast and their friends from the Broadway spectacular he had seen earlier were celebrating their successful opening night. That was when he met his Maria.

His financial extravagance brought a seductive light to her eyes as superficial as his feelings for her. Neither ever spoke about their real feelings. She didn't ask where he went when not with her, nor did he question her about where she invested her time when they were apart. Sufficient were the days when he came to town, and she dropped everything to give him her full dark-eyed attention.

The affair proved a potent motivation for Taylor to slip additional top secret patents to the man who paid immediately and abundantly. While his actress mistress played her roles on Broadway, Taylor played deeper into his fantasy. Onassis had made his fortune through a series of businesses, some of which had hardly been moral or ethical. Heady with his emerging secret life, Taylor played a larger game. One that would free him to devote all his time to the pursuits that pleased him.

His chance came in the form of a patent for a revolutionary new jet engine. Like Onassis, he negotiated. The day his secret account received a deposit for more money than he dreamed he would have, Taylor retired. Retired from his job at the USPTO, and retired from his mundane, middle-class life.

Under the guise of a consulting business, he frequented New York for the periodic rendezvous with Maria. This evening his wife thought Taylor traveled for work. But, in fact, fully Aristotle, he took in the clear evening sky and the view of the harbor from the roof of the New York apartment he provided for his mistress. In that magic span of time between day and night, the lights twinkled on, and the city changed from work clothes to evening attire.

With her dramatic flare, the actress had set the stage on the open-air patio with soft music and a low dining table. Waiting for their favorite chef to send up a meal, he lounged on a Cleopatra-style bed, thick with throws and pillows, watching the sultry actress give him a private showing of her upcoming role. He planned to arrange their next tryst in a new, exotic setting. First Monaco, then Paris. He smiled. The future beckoned with an unlimited variety of places to practice being a wealthy playboy.

With a mechanical hiss, the elevator door opened, and the delivery man arrived carrying carefully packed dishes smelling of coconut and curry. The pack strapped on the delivery man's back surely held their chilled champagne.

The waiter arranged the dishes and placed silverware.

Taylor crossed to the table, reaching for his wallet to give the expected tip.

"Sir, is this to your liking?" The waiter gestured to the table, inviting Taylor to inspect the product.

Certainly, a step up from meatloaf Tuesdays and spaghetti Wednesdays, Taylor lifted the lid of a silver dish, noted the bright vegetables, and breathed in the steamy aroma.

Suddenly, the waiter grabbed Taylor from behind. In a single movement, his arms were pulled behind his back and plastic handcuffs bound his wrists. Muscled to the edge of the patio by the waiter, he heard Maria shriek. A tight cord quickly pinned Taylor to his abductor. Taylor's back pressed against the man's hard chest.

Over Maria's scream came the whop, whop of a helicopter. As the chopper bore down on them, Taylor's abductor pulled a cord attached to the pack on his back. Instead of the expected bubbly champagne, a short high pitch whine followed a whiplash jerk. A parachute blew heavenward as if shot from a cannon, carrying the two men straight up.

A helicopter banked around and somehow grabbed the parachute. Another jerk, stronger than the first, and he swung away from his fantasy and from his Maria. The wind took his breath, and his feet kicked the air over the concrete streets and buildings passing rapidly beneath him. In that instant, he knew nothing like this had ever happened to Aristotle Onassis.

After all the business opportunities, all the money, all the hours with his mistress, he could no longer pretend to live the life of the legendary Greek tycoon. He was just Arnold Taylor. And he was in trouble.

Chapter Ninety-four

Marc grabbed Lei's hand and pulled her to a hiding place near the door. "It's gonna get loud and dangerous. When the guards come looking, I want you out of the way." Opening a metal locker, he ushered her inside. "Stay here."

Before he could change his own mind, Marc jogged to the machine and initiated the sequence for simultaneous explosions at the same time the city fireworks would begin. The noise he made inside would not be detected as quickly with everyone's attention on the pyrotechnics. Anything visual from the lab would be camouflaged by the light of the official display aimed over the water outside the building.

He must act now or never, and Marc chose now. With a deafening sound, the outburst felt like being inside a Fourth of July display. Dodging sparks and debris, Marc pressed himself out of sight.

With a start, the sleeping guard jumped to his feet as the second guard groggily stumbled through the door. Both men held their guns, searching for a target. Yelling, the two raced forward into the acrid smoke, searching and calling for Marc and the hidden Lei.

Marc saw his chance and slipped out the door behind them. He turned away from his usual route to and from the lab, knowing nothing lay between the lab and his living quarters that would do him any good. He had no idea what lay at the opposite end except the security men Lei had warned him about.

"There are a lot of weapons," Lei had told him. That sounded promising. Right now, he could use the American cavalry or at least a sturdy tank.

Dashing down the wide hall, Marc panicked. Hearing something amiss, two guards were running toward him. Looking back, he saw light flash through the smoke that billowed from the lab. The building shook as more explosions rocked the foundations.

Yelling, the guards drew their guns and rushed upon him. At that moment, Marc began yelling and pointing to the laboratory.

"You think you can kidnap whoever you want," he hollered. "There!" He pointed back to where he had come. "There's your new weapon. I hope you all go to hell with it."

From the lab, a guard emerged, staggering and coughing. Choking, he gulped in a great lungful of air. The two soldiers who had just come upon the scene looked from their collapsed comrade to Marc.

"You people are crazy." Marc waved his arms in expansive circles at the noise and smoke pouring toward them. More words tumbled out, hysterical gibberish spewed from his mouth like the panorama bursting forth in the lab.

Large black boots thundered past him. Stunned, Marc watched the soldiers run into the smoking laboratory. Surprised that his captors neither shot nor corralled him back into a locked cell, Marc seized the opportunity and bolted down the hall in the direction the two armed men had just come from.

Chapter Ninety-five

A set of double doors, much like the ones that closed off the lab, stood before Marc. Without an option to turn back, he possessed limited time. From his pocket he fished the name badge manufactured with Hebron's ingenuity and pressed the image to the scanner. The door opened. In that instant, Marc promised himself that if he managed to return home, he would bring in the random-thinking redhead student inventor as some kind of business partner.

Inside the cavernous room, Marc surveyed a well-organized system. Military weapons were neatly arranged. Shipping boxes sat on sawhorses. Half were sealed closed, lettering in different languages printed on the sides. Others were packed with weapons but topless. One row of crates remained empty. The Chinese, Marc observed, were involved in several businesses including shipping illegal arms to foreign entities. What a surprise. While a hunch, Marc doubted any of the shipments went to allies of the United States.

From an open crate, Marc quickly lifted a Lightweight Anti-Tank Weapon. Not much more than a strengthened fiberglass tube, the LAW was designed to shoot once and then be discarded. Dr. Thurmond collected World War II militaria. From a gun show, the two had brought home an expended launcher that Marc had converted into an air-soft weapon. Though provided by the Chinese, these copies of a US weapon would appear to be supplied by the United States. Arm America's enemies, and if the illegal shipments were intercepted, the US looked bad in a win-win arrangement for China.

With this one-shot firearm, Marc held a single opportunity to use the M72 LAW. At five-and-a-half pounds each, he slung two over his right shoulder to rest against his back. A third he hung over his left shoulder, the canister across his chest. They were cold. Shifting his body weight to accommodate the load, he hoisted a fourth launcher in his hands and raced back to the laboratory.

The guard who had staggered outside of the lab lay in the hall in a fetal position. Marc couldn't tell if he still breathed and didn't care as long as the man couldn't harm Marc or Lei. One down. Somewhere in the smoke and debris were three men who would like to find him.

"It's either you or me." Dropping to one knee, he shouldered the weapon he carried, aimed, and pulled the trigger.

A raucous blast and the ancient structure's far wall ruptured and collapsed. As the dust cleared, he tossed away the used LAW. From his right shoulder, he retrieved a second launcher, aimed, and fired again. Satisfied he made a hole sufficiently large enough for his machine to have flown through, he ran toward the opening he had just created.

Something caught him by the ankle, and Marc came down hard, his face smashing into the ground. Powerful hands rolled him over and began to pummel his body. Before he could react, his attacker connected a powerful fist with a missile launcher strung across Marc's middle. The man screamed with pain. With all his might, Marc swung the empty launcher he still grasped and slammed his assailant across the temple. The guard rolled to the floor. Marc rose up on one knee and swung the weapon wild a second time at the rushing attacker. Smashing the man's cheekbone, the blow sent him to the ground, blood pooling around his face.

Scrambling to his feet, Marc hurried to the far side of the

building where his two missiles had done their work. A military boot, the foot still inside, lay caught on the jagged edge of the opening. Marc dropped the empty LAW as bile rose in his throat. Catching his breath, he tore his eyes away from the grizzly sight. One guard out of commission in the hall, one bleeding on the ground, and a third had been unfortunate to be in the path of one of his missile shots. Three down.

Outdoors, the fresh air thrilled his senses. Marc realized he hadn't seen the outside world in a terribly long time. Midwest winters were infamous for weeks of skies in what Mallory termed Indiana-gray. The nickname described a color as distinct as Payne's gray and cadmium orange were to a portrait artist. Seeing the immenseness of the long-missed horizon in the twilight took his breath away. He blinked several times and squinted to absorb the sight. Before him lay the world's largest cargo port in the emerging global city.

Lei had said they were in Shanghai. The vast body of water that flowed past the ancient temple-turned-military-development-complex would be the mouth of the Yangtze. The tang of salt sea air assured him that the broad body of the East China Sea lay beyond. And then the Pacific Ocean. The same Pacific Ocean that caressed the West Coast of the United States, half a world away. China had been an exotic destination on the opposite side of the globe. A place Marc had planned to visit.

"Not exactly how I planned to get here." There were a number of sites he had anticipated touring. Modern Pudong with its Oriental Pearl Tower, the historic and renovated Bund, and City God Temple. "Not this trip."

He took in his surroundings and made quick calculations. Charging back to the Meissner Device, he examined it like a pool shark considers the perfect angle for a combo. Drawing a third weapon, Marc fired the missile launcher. As hoped, the explosive tore into his project with enormous force and propelled the largest part of the machine through the newly blasted outlet. Like a wounded falcon, the Meissner Device convulsed over the opaque Yangtze and slammed into the unforgiving water. Hot from the explosion, the shattered pieces sizzled and groaned, listed sideways, and vanished below the surface.

Turning, Marc saw Lei behind him. Fear showed on her face, but she wasn't looking at the water. Following her line of vision, he spotted a guard aiming his sidearm at Marc's head.

"Zhi!" Lei's cry distracted the man for the split-second Marc needed. Screaming at the top of his lungs, he ducked and ran straight at the gunman. A gunshot rang out, and Marc felt fire along his left shoulder that spun him like a top. The momentum carried him around a second time, and he swung the empty launcher like Babe Ruth at bat. The weapon caught the gunman across the chest. Grunting as the air was knocked from his lungs, the guard fired a wild shot from his pistol. Mustering all his strength, Marc swung the launcher again. This time he connected with the man's jaw and heard the sickening sound of crushing bone.

With a nightmarish yell drowned in blood collecting in his throat, the man whirled like a kite without a tail. Teeth falling from his mouth, he slammed into a workstation and slid to the floor.

Breathing hard, Marc dropped the empty launcher tube that also served as a baseball bat. He mounted a forklift and dragged the residual section of his creation through the hole in the building and unceremoniously dumped the contents into the filthy harbor. In moments, the mangled machinery disappeared under the dark surface, a string of bubbles marking the descent. Beside him, Lei tossed the expended LAWs she had gathered into the Yangtze.

Retrieving the last launcher, he carefully aimed above the hole with the intent to cause the most structural damage and fired. The ancient building shuddered, and large sections cascaded down. Marc threw the launcher, bloody from his shoulder wound, into the water outside where the weapon quickly disappeared under the swirling current.

In the distance, came the tinny sound of sirens. He figured the fireworks had bought him some time, but despite the distraction, the neighbors had noticed the noise, the smoke, strange happenings along the water, or all three. Would Colonel Yao be on his way?

Running back from the destruction, Marc grabbed Lei's wrist. "Come on, we gotta go!"

Urgently, he pulled her back along the hallway and into the weapons room. He took her to a 48 by 48 by 84-inch box on a footprint pallet that Marc guessed were positioned to ship out next. A drill lay nearby ready for the next day's work. Quickly, Marc bored breathing holes where they would not be immediately noticed.

Turning to Lei, he saw she was trembling. His hands on her slender shoulders, he steadied her and looked intently into her eyes. "It's okay for you to go back. No one will blame you. You will be safe." He waved an arm at the pallet behind him. "This is a risk you don't have to take. Now go!"

She gritted her teeth to stop their nervous chattering and clenched her fists against the involuntary quaking. "I'm going with you."

With no more time to argue, Marc lifted Lei into his arms and set her inside an empty crate. "Lay down," he ordered. "Stay still and be quiet. Act like a crate full of missile launchers."

Her eyes large with excitement and fright, she did exactly as told. "What about you?"

He hooked a thumb at the nearby crate. "I'm dressing up like a load of AK-47s." Marc reached for the propane driven nail gun and secured the lid into place to resemble the other packed crates.

He double-checked that Lei was safely packed and climbed into his own wooden box. Pulling the top until the piece dropped into place, he felt for the nail gun he'd brought inside. In the cramped quarters, he managed to crate himself securely inside what he gambled would be their transport to freedom.

Chapter Ninety-six

Yao struggled to appear calm. To maintain control. He had been enjoying his second gin and the attention of a lovely woman at a formal celebration event for those of his political station when an aide discreetly whispered that something unexplained appeared to be taking place at the lab.

He hurried back to the temple, and like countless times before, entered the main door. But unlike other visits, the ancient building's tang of age and incense had been replaced with an odor of battlefield explosives. Outside the lab, medical personnel hoisted an unconscious guard onto a stretcher. Inside, the Colonel stepped over the still body of another guard and rudely pushed through the stunned workers blocking his path. His gaze went first to the large hole in the wall, then to the empty area at the room's center.

The bodies of two guards lay in unnatural positions, and someone with a medical bag bent over the nearest.

Touching the blackened floor, he rubbed the ash between thumb and middle fingers. He circled the perimeter of the large burned mark. Last, he examined the hole through the exterior wall. A hole large enough to fly the device through. The others stood still, waiting.

Had the inventor blasted through the wall to provide an exit for the machine? Where would he go? How far could the Meissner Device travel? Or was there another explanation in the destruction? While working under Yao's observation, Marc Wayne had procured a means of escape. And he took the device with him.

Furiously, he barked orders. Personnel jumped and scurried from the room. Clenching his fists at his sides, Yao marched back to the door where he turned to slowly survey the large laboratory where he had invested his time and influence in recent years. He swore loudly, the angry words echoing in the hollows of the previously bustling center of new technology.

In the hall, men assembled for his instructions. "Divide into teams. Search the building." He glanced at the river through the opening in the far wall. "Search outside. Search everywhere."

He gave orders to notify other government and military personnel to be on the lookout on land and above the ground.

Then he summoned the scientists. They arrived from various points in the city where families were celebrating National Day. Stunned by what they saw, each entered the lab and slowly tip-toed through the debris, trying to make sense of what had happened. Looking like ashamed puppies, they gathered before Yao.

"Study his notes." Disdain dripping from his words, he wanted them to comprehend his disappointment in their lack of achievement. "Find out how he made this work!"

Chapter Ninety-seven

His box was being pried open. Marc wasn't certain how long he had been cramped in the small rectangle, but he felt desperate for water. He squirmed, trying to encourage blood flow to his numb feet. Cramped, different parts of his body had taken turns screaming in agony during the transport. Mercifully, a few areas eventually lost feeling due to pinched circulation. Not as courteous, his neck, shoulders, and hips screamed with pain.

With a final snap, the wooden lid broke open, and Marc squeezed his eyes closed against the sudden rush of blinding sunlight.

"Son of a…" the oath seamlessly streamed into another language that Marc guessed to be Arabic. He recognized *cheekia*, slang for guns. And *dhimmi*, a word meaning Christian set apart for religious tolerance by the Koran.

Someone roughly grabbed his shirtfront and jerked Marc upright. Spasms wracked his legs with searing pain. Dragged out of the box and to his feet, Marc wobbled weak-kneed and keenly aware of an AK-47 pressed painfully into his ribs.

Thank you for reading *The Patent*. We appreciate sharing the adventures of Marc and Mallory Wayne with you.

If you have a moment, please leave a review on Amazon at www.amazon.com. Reviews are the best gift you gift an author.

Book 2 in the Marc Wayne Adventure series by P.S. Wells and Max Garwood is titled *Gun Runner*.

The prequel to *The Patent* is *Chasing Sunrise* by P.S. Wells, available in e-book, paperback, and in a dramatic audio version.

Other titles you may like by P.S. Wells include:

- *Chasing Sunrise*
- *Homeless for the Holidays*
- Check out the audio version of *Homeless for the Holidays* read by voice actress Katie Leigh
- *The Ten Best Decisions A Single Mom Can Make*
- *Slavery in the Land of the Free*
- *The Girl Who Wore Freedom*

Connect with P.S. Wells at www.PeggySueWells.com. I'd love to hear from you.

Made in the USA
Middletown, DE
03 October 2023